MY INFLATABLE FRIEND

MY INFLATABLE FRIEND
THE CONFESSIONS OF ROLLO HEMPHILL

GERALD EVERETT JONES

LaPuerta
Books and Media
www.lapuerta.tv

Copyright © 2007 by Gerald Everett Jones

Excerpts: Preface © 2022, Boychik Lit © 2013, Rubber Babes © 2008

All rights reserved.

No part of this book may be reproduced in any form or by any electronic or mechanical means, including information storage and retrieval systems, without written permission from the author, except for the use of brief quotations in a book review.

LaPuerta Books and Media

Email: bookstore@lapuerta.tv

Fan blog: geraldeverettjones.com

The characters and events of this story are fictitious; any resemblance to actual persons, living or dead, is entirely coincidental.

TRADEMARKS: The author has attempted throughout this book to distinguish proprietary trademarks from descriptive terms by following the capitalization style used by the trademark owner. Any product trademarks, service marks, and registered trademarks appearing herein are the properties of their respective owners and are hereby acknowledged.

EPUB ISBN: 978-0-9794866-7-8

LaPuerta softcover print edition ISBN: 978-0-9794866-1-6

Editors: Trent Babington, Jason Letts

Cover design by Blinky, 100covers.com

LaPuerta is an imprint of La Puerta Productions https://lapuerta.tv, Santa Monica, California, USA

For Cheerful Charlie

PREFACE

When the notion of reissuing Rollo Hemphill's misadventures floated past in my stream of consciousness, my next thought was, *Hey, those stories are evergreen — why not?* But more practical considerations of the publishing marketplace prevailed, necessitating this explanatory note.

My concern isn't that the characters won't be relatable or their follies any less funny in the glare of freshly fired-up high-wattage attention. No, the problem is one of perceived technological obsolescence. The first novel in the series — *My Inflatable Friend* — was released in 2007. To some of you in the shivering audience for whom first impressions can be cool if not downright cold, that era might not seem so long ago. But to others, the crusty tale might as well have occurred just before the undocumented end of the last Ice Age. (There have been more than one, I'm told. Hence the rush to print again, lest the next big freeze overtake us. Hmm. Some in fire, some in ice. We probably don't get to pick.)

When the first novel in the series was released, cell phones existed but weren't yet what you'd call smart. Email was a thing, surely, but social media had not yet turned the world's great newspapers into ezines for old folks.

Some Luddites still clung to their fax (facsimile) machines, especially those who insisted that electronic signature was an oxymoron.

Some movie crews who were filming were still actually using film. Likewise for shows taping.

Into this latter-day Age of Innocence schlepped poor Rollo, whose challenges getting attention from females, then avoiding journalists and G-men, could no doubt have been helped by the option of sending the occasional exculpatory text message. Emojis wouldn't have hurt his cause either, and an amusing animation, especially if cloned onto his bodily image as a wisecracking avatar, might have put him right over the top. (Or on the bottom. At the outset, positional advantage was far from his foremost concern.)

Back then, climate change could have been mitigated — or didn't exist — depending on which talking head you credited. In fact, "the end of the world as we know it" was mostly a worn-out sci-fi theme, hardly a topic of almost unremitting daily conversation. A pandemic was a post-WWI episode, not feared to be repeated because threats such as Ebola and AIDS had presumably been contained. The James Bond movie franchise was still going strong because male guilt, belatedly dredged up by #MeToo, had not yet made it necessary (spoiler alert!) to kill the legendary rapist off.

And — perhaps most significant for the sake of Rollo's first episode — lifelike robots designed for intimate uses may have been in development but were certainly not yet ready for the likes of Rollo.

Mind you, Rollo's stories need not be read in sequence. *Rubber Babes* exists in its own quirky paranoid reality, and *Farnsworth's Revenge* is no less sweet when not saved for last, but the through-line of Rollo's lurching character development does flow in a bobbing chronology through these books. Wise readers will know better than to regard him as a role model. Rollo's problem — if you insist on calling it that — is paradoxical: No matter what scheme he tries or how it fails — he persists in falling ever-upward.

I could wonder, though, whether male-centered comic humor can be written anymore. Men seem more pathetic than funny now, as do some who oddly claim to be both white and marginalized. *Satire* might still be a useful term, but nowadays its connotations tend to be political. Rollo does get enmeshed in complications on an international scale — but he has no agenda other than self-preservation.

My original inspiration for these novels was my admiration for the novelist and poet Peter De Vries. In the mid-twentieth century, his male-centered comic novels ridiculed religion and extramarital sex — often in the same book. However, the whiff of controversy, so delicious in his day, has not aged well, and some would say positively reeks. In *Forever Panting* (my favorite), an out-of-work actor divorces his wife and marries his mother-in-law, continuing to lust after his ex. In *Slouching Toward Kalamazoo,* a female high-school teacher carries on an affair with her tender-aged male student.

Such themes are not exactly fodder for popular humor these days.

Lest you think I'm preoccupied with peters, I'll confess that the works of Peter Lefcourt also influenced me. *The Woody* is brilliant, and by virtue of its inside-the-Beltway setting, it qualifies as legitimately political satire. (Alas, whether Lefcourt was satirizing Gary Hart or Bill Clinton or both is a question not likely to be explored by any contemporary book club.) And he wrote *Eleven Karens* when it was still possible to bestow the name on a newborn girl.

As well, when I began to stir the pot of silliness on my own, the publishing business had finally been taken over by women — along with the belated recognition that, for decades if not since Gutenberg, the most avid readers have been women. The genre chick-lit had come full flower. Appreciating the polar opposites such as De Vries and Lefcourt, I coined the term *boychik lit* as a lodestar for sinking ships helmed by ill-fated peters.

So, by way of further explanation — as if any more of my rants were needed to cheer you on to root for Rollo — I append my essay "Boychik Lit" at the end of this volume.

Thank you for the use of the genre. If Rollo's exploits bring a smile, you needn't tell anyone.

Gerald Everett Jones
Santa Monica - June, 2022

CHAPTER 1
MY CONFESSION

My name is Rollo Hemphill and I'm no pervert. This little book is the story of what I did with my inflatable friend, and the mostly embarrassing consequences accruing therefrom. As to the details of what I did, I refuse to bottom-line them until you know me better. Please keep an open mind and grant me a few pages by way of exculpatory background before I spill it, which I assure you I did, must, and will do.

Don't read too much into it, this compulsion to confess my sorry deeds. You might surmise I had to write this as some punitive form of public service, and rather than deny that ugly accusation, I simply won't say. If I gave you that up front, it would beg a host of other awkward questions, such as how and on what charge I was apprehended, how my public defender screwed the pooch and reamed me, and how society takes a warped view of even the purest and simplest of natural human urges. In short, if I copped to all that now, I'd be giving away the ending, and every Lit 101 student knows it's hard enough figuring out how to finish a first-person narrative without tipping off the reader on the first page.

But trust me. Let me apply some backstory by way of lubricant, and I promise you'll get the whole thing in the end.

Way back when the root of all evil had not yet begun to flower, I was working as a car jockey at the Wuthering Palms Hotel. How, my old friends might ask, does an Exeter man find himself in such a menial position? I was lucky. My hacking career had been going so well that if I had not sent that self-incriminating email to the Feds, today I'd be doing a long stretch in Leavenworth. Too clever for my own good. Story of my life.

It was my Apple got me in trouble, and it didn't fall far from the tree. My father is supposedly in Costa Rica somewhere, something about a hedge fund or junk bonds, maybe both. My mother has the house in Darien all to herself, grows prize roses, and drinks a lot of "tea." What passes for her philosophy of parenting holds that if you can't say anything nice, don't say anything at all — so we never speak.

Long story shortened to not even a story, the Feds took away my encryption chip and made me swear I'd hacked my last, and, okay, I did some time. But they expunged my record because I was a month under eighteen when I let myself get caught. (By the way, I literally dropped out of Exeter. I leaped from a window after curfew, and they locked me out for good.)

At last, here I am parking cars at the Palms and thinking myself damn fortunate to have my very own legit Social Security number for once and a day job I can tell my friends about. If I ever have any.

On one of those dazzlingly bright California mornings that make rednecks back East flush with jealousy every year when they tune into the Rose Parade, I was thinking myself particularly smart to be out for a spin down Sunset in the Rolls Silver Cloud. (It's the property of a guest who was booked into one of our bungalows for an extended stay.) Now, here is one of the few cars on the planet designed to optimize the ride in the *back* seat, and it being such a fine day, the sunroof open and the sweet scents of eucalyptus and jasmine in the air, my imagination naturally turned to wondering how many bare behinds had been caressed by that buttery-soft calfskin as upright conduct was driven ardently home to them while the chauffeur did his own driving home trying his damnedest to keep his curious, beady eyes on the road. I mean, what's the point of owning the most luxurious car in the world if it doesn't get you laid? (Attention span: *Think* of the boost you'd get from the throb of the turbines in a corporate jet!)

Thinking it pointless to concentrate on sex for very long unless it's in the same room with me, I deliberately turned my attention to the incredible ride, the physical sensation of controlling the old gal, for all her hulk and heft. In this latter-day era of McPherson struts, rack and pinion steering, and computer-mitigated everything, the Silver Cloud is a miracle of traditional, conservatively bred elegance in motion. In the jaunty bounce-bounce of her coil and semi-elliptic springs, the saucy pump-pump of her silky pistons, her reciprocating ball joint — she has nothing remotely new, just standup workmanship in heavy metal. She held her course like a planet-sized rock hurtling through airless space, and if any of her old joints were the slightest bit loose from all those years of bumping and grinding, she gave not a whimper of protest. Oh, you Brits, you stuck-up, hedonistic hypocrites — you built a banker's fuckmobile!

I'm obsessed with sex. Isn't that normal?

As a matter of continuing education for potential career advancement, I was prone to using these little spins, supplemented by otherwise idle time spent in parked cars, to practice my improvisational skills as a shock-jock deejay. Perhaps because I hadn't scored in a lizard's lifetime, I was going through a Blue Period, trying for Howard Stern but with more edge. Personally, I would just as soon listen to real blues or even bluegrass at such times, but the voiceover style I was attempting was more like a heavy-metal shitstorm tantrum. Grabbing an empty bottle of Evian from the floorboard to use as a mic, I let fly:

"It's Rockin' Rollo the Rocknroller in the ER — electroshock radio — where we just keep shovin' it atcha. That was 'Can't Get No More' by the Skin Lollipops. Super-ficial! Next up, pud-whackers, it's number seven on the charts, 'Gotta Getcha' by the Road Warriors. It's goin' out to Felicia from you-know-who, who's you know what — gotta getcha!"

I can give 'em raw, if that's what it takes. No sooner did I end my rant than the blues wafted over me for real. It's not so much that I didn't like what I did. My stylings, the inflections, the energy — the whole glib patter thing — was okay technically. I just didn't like myself when I was doing it.

It helps the realism to be able to fade the music down going into the patter and up coming out of it, but if I'm driving and holding the mic, I don't have a hand free to work my iPod. I could lose the mic, but my ego needed the prop.

The circuitous route of my mentations and motoring brought me eventually to the portals of my employer. I eased the old gal into the Palms and brought her to rest ostentatiously under the arch in the circular drive at the prestigious guest entrance.

My blood up from the stimulation of the ride, I leapt out with elan, looking every bit the playboy, I hoped, in my crested blazer, knife-edged gabardine trousers, open-neck crêpe-de-Chine shirt, and Morocco slip-ons (all celebrity castoffs from Goodwill). Tossing my silk scarf rakishly over one shoulder, I strode confidently down the welcoming red carpet, wanting to give the impression of a valued guest in an important hurry.

My way was blocked oafishly by Laszlo, our exceptionally short Hungarian doorman, who apparently did not understand his role in the script and instead of enhancing my image by making straight my way, interposed his diminutive, plump self dumbly between me and the door.

"Later, Laszlo," I uttered with an aristocratic air as I shoved him gently but firmly aside, striving to maintain my forward momentum. He looked as though he were about to speak, which I noted with an ill-timed turn of my head, as I entered the huge revolving glass door. Whether he were about to caution me about some defect in the door mechanism or simply wanted to wish me a nice day, I never found out, because my looking back combined with my forward motion had the effect of lifting my scarf in the breeze of the door's whirl, causing the tassels to lodge inconveniently between the door and the jamb, halting its rapid revolution, trapping me inside, constricting my neck, and very nearly choking me to death.

Perhaps confused about my intentions and not quick enough to prevent the mishap, Laszlo nevertheless bravely hurtled his small self to the rescue and began tugging furiously on the door. This must have been the opposite of the required action, because the door froze with a terrifying squeak, the scarf stretched tighter, and I could feel the blood rushing to my anguished face.

Pleading through the glass at the balding little man, my cries made no sound, for I could summon no air to stir my vocal cords. Instinctively, I strained my head to the end of its tether, which only served to wedge me in tighter and further constrict my windpipe. Laszlo's worried face began to dissolve into a blissful pink cloud, and just as I was going under, I heard him exclaim, "Some big shot! Pullingk ven he should be —"

He must have decided then and there he'd be the one to change direction and threw all his hundred pounds at me.

" — Pushingk!" I heard his exasperated cough as the door gave way, spinning me inside, loosening the stranglehold, granting me a glorious, dizzying gulp of air, and throwing me onto the ornate splendor of the Persian rug in the lobby with little Laszlo on top of me looking pathetically like a Pomeranian trying to hump a Great Dane.

With remarkable grace, I thought, he rolled off me, stood, retrieved his billed cap, and fastidiously brushed his uniform, finishing by dusting off the gilt epaulets. Adjusting his cap and straightening his tie, he looked down at me, an unusual angle for him. "Some big shot," he muttered, then turned and waltzed back through the ill-designed door to resume his post at the curb.

With a weak smile of grateful appreciation and trying to suppress the idea I'd just had intimate bodily contact with a homely, short man, I stood slowly, expecting my pratfall had made me the humorous butt of the assembled crowd in the busy hotel lobby.

To my amazement, no one was watching. Not that the place was empty — far from it. There must have been fifty people in there, but my entrance hadn't drawn the slightest attention. Instead, all eyes were on a half-dozen television screens strategically located at conversational gathering points in the large room.

One glance at a monitor told me there was no use competing with the most famous pair of tits in Hollywood.

Monica LaMonica, her cleavage cut so low you wondered how physical support was achieved, puckered up to plant a big, wet, passionate one on Buck Morehead, her leading hunk du jour. Ignoring the fact that such immodest décolletage was not the practice in the antebellum South, Monica's costumers had her in ringlet curls, a velvet choker with a heart-shaped diamond setting off her ivory throat. Conveniently for the sake of historical accuracy on his part, Dick wore nothing above the waist but a gleaming coat of coconut oil.

Must be a fantasy sequence, I thought — knowing well, along with the rest of the free world, that *The Edge of Endlessness* is a contemporary Upper East Side melodrama centering on the engrossing peccadilloes of gorgeous and conniving professionals in today's fast-paced, cutthroat media industry.

Realizing that my cover had not been blown, I sauntered over to the bar with a renewed air of overconfidence, there to greet Nigel, our redoubtable concierge, who was sipping a Midori neat, totally out of keeping with company policy about drinking on the job.

"What's the big deal?" I asked him.

He shushed me, indicating the screen. "Jessica is going to tell Courtenay he's history."

"Not before he tells her he's got a week to live."

"That's impossible. His transplant took. You out sick yesterday?"

I couldn't take any more. "Why doesn't *she* get the disease of the week?" I wondered, knowing it was a ridiculous question. Turning from the screen, I spied a copy of *Loose Lips* on the bar.

Four-walling her fame, as the publicists in this town would say, Monica's color picture was on the front page of the tabloid. Above her trademark heart-shaped sunglasses and profusion of red hair, the headline read: "MONICA LaMONICA — SHE WANTS TO BE ALONE!"

Perhaps too loudly, I asked Nigel or no one, "When was she ever alone?"

"We're telling them she's in the south of France."

"I see London, I see France. I bet we're washing her underpants."

He sneered as if I were some disloyal footman and went back to watching the steamy episode.

Having spotted her stretch limo on the lot just moments ago, I had a pretty good idea where I would find the hotel's most notorious secret resident. I had another, more urgent reason to go there, so, resuming my air of bored nobility, I set off across the expansive lobby toward the beauty shop.

An older couple perched on a settee in the center of the room. (My guess was third-generation German from Milwaukee — lousy tippers.) He had a camcorder slung around his neck and a *Map of the Stars' Homes* stuffed in a thick Michener paperback. All he needed was a placard: "TOURIST CARRIES $500 IN TRAVELERS' CHECKS." Out of the corner of my eye, I could see the two of them scoping me, assessing my St. Tropez look and self-important walk, wondering *who I am.*

Good question, I think.

The reception area of the beauty shop was empty and dark. Opening the inside door to the workstations, I caught my heart's desire in an innocently erotic pose.

Felicia Ferrulo, a gorgeous, dark, hot-blooded lady whose ancestors must surely have been Sicilian, was bent over a draped woman in the chair. Felicia's back was toward me, and her micro-mini had hiked up so the plump bottoms of her sweet cheeks peeked out, separated by a small wedge of hot-pink undies with lace trim.

Enthralled in the moment, I took a long, deep breath. Felicia! If she had given me a tumble then, *all this would not have been necessary.*

I expected to find Monica in Felicia's chair, but it was another guest, one who was rich enough but fameless. At that moment, Ms. LaMonica was probably safely installed in our Bungalow B, where she'd registered last week as "Jayne Jones — Inquiries to Manager." She had quickly developed a fondness for Felicia, who in her capacity as caregiver was a trusted member of the star's life-support team. My contact with our stellar guest had been limited to opening her car door now and then, and my own survival sense told me to keep it that way.

Not finding the star there made me bolder. "Babe, we are gonna be so fantastic," I muttered, thinking about kissing the moist lips under the pink wedgie.

Felicia paid no attention and turned to wash her gooey hands in the sink. Thinking I was still unnoticed, I walked up behind her and reached for the moon. But before I could make contact, my wrist was stopped and clamped tight as an iron manacle.

Her pouty face turned toward me now, and I grew all the more excited seeing she was flushed and sweaty from her labors. Her nails dug into my wrist as her wet-look rouged lips formed a sensuous, sneering French pucker. She blew a puff of air upward, dislodging a damp, dangling curl from her noble, perspiring forehead. "What we have is not necessarily a relationship, and my name's not Babe."

I distinctly remember starting to say, "We need to talk. I'll drop by tonight with a bottle of Chateau —"

"No, you won't," Felicia said, cutting me off as she closed the door behind me.

Oh! I would walk on hot coals for this woman, but she knew I was already cooked, and she was not having any.

CHAPTER 2
SHOT DOWN

Dante had his Beatrice. For me it's Felicia. Not only is the object of my desire heart-stoppingly beautiful herself, but she can also create beauty. As a qualified Sassoon graduate, she knows her scissor work and razor cuts, her lotions and mudpacks, her depilatories, dyes, and balms. Unfortunately for my span of attention on anything else but her, I see her every day at the Palms.

Ah! (Knuckle bite.)

She said we didn't, but we had a relationship to speak of — that is, we were on speaking terms. She'd rushed me out of her shop today, but usually she didn't seem to mind my stopping by on my break. She'd talk as she worked, sometimes even directly to me. (It sounded like singing, I thought.) I would listen and try to think of charming and witty rejoinders, but mostly I just stared in awe. She was genuine second-generation Italian, with that cappuccino-colored Mediterranean skin, jet-black hair worn in a passionate tease, red pouty lips that said "You don't own me" (but dared you to die trying), and that little bead of sweat on her upper lip when she got steamed — which happened when she expressed herself forcefully, as she often did with characteristic Sicilian zeal. Many were the times I fantasized about that little string of sweat beads breaking out in the hot throes of physical passion induced by my ardent thrusting.

Ah!

Undeterred and having rehearsed my speech before the mirror at home, I dropped 'round to her place as promised. I carried a chilled bottle of Dom (borrowed from a room-service tray — I don't make that kind of money). I sported a velour sweat suit — a comfortable, package-flattering ensemble that could be shucked quickly, I pictured, for that long-awaited, hastily consummated romp in her bedroom.

The apartment door swung open graciously at my buzzing to reveal her, drop-dead gorgeous in a floor-length silk evening gown with pendant earrings. Although I'm sure I mentioned earlier that day I'd be paying a visit, I hadn't said anything about stepping out, especially in such style. So there we were — she dressed for the ballroom at the Ritz, me for pizza and TV, albeit with a respectable sparkling wine.

No matter. We'd both be undressed soon enough, hiccuping and giggling at the oddity and delight of lovers' first coupling.

A puzzled look passed over her face like a wispy cloud temporarily hiding the sun. "Rollo, that's right. You said you had something to ask me, but I didn't think you meant you'd be showing up, uh, here."

If not now, not ever. "I was just wondering whether you'd be interested in getting married. To me, I mean."

The little cloud became a thunderhead and shot a bolt into her brain. I thought she stumbled back, but maybe she just blinked.

"You'd better come in," she said numbly.

It was the first time I'd been to her place. The walls were filled with her paintings, the exclusive subject matter of which was puppies staring out with abnormally large, watery, affectionate eyes. Apparently, my love was the Keane of canine portraiture.

Ah, there was so much more about her I would learn, and eagerly!

She didn't invite me to sit, didn't offer a beverage or snack. In fact, she seemed disoriented in her own house. I stood frozen, holding the bottle of Dom behind my back.

Will she guess I swiped it?

She turned her head away (to wipe a tear?) and on turning back said, "I didn't see this coming, Rollo. People usually, I don't know, *date* first."

"I'm new at this," was all I could find to say, playing the Fool card of naivete, since worldliness obviously wasn't my strong suit.

From somewhere within herself she summoned fire, and I got a flash of my mother's nine-pound Pekingese Shotzi, who quickly bites male dogs of any size squarely on the nose as they approach. Neither of these gals need ever fear a Rottweiler in a dark alley.

As abruptly as I'd popped the question, she turned me down, and, ignoring the implications on the duration of my visit or my life's entire future course, I dumbly asked for the reasons why.

"Why *would I* marry you is a much shorter list," she explained carefully. "Let's keep this positive.

"You're cute and sweet," she continued, "and you have a nice sense of humor when you let yourself relax." This girl didn't have any trouble expressing herself, a trait I really admired, even as I was stung by the sharp truth of her list, not to mention its conciseness. I waited for her to go on, but she didn't.

"But why *don't* you...?" I couldn't help it coming out as a whine.

Her glance flitted from her watch to a wall clock, and I was impressed that she would bother to synchronize them, especially at this moment.

She became impatient and apparently decided to break her own rule about avoiding criticism. "For one thing, you're unfocused."

"I turned a corner in my life today," I protested. "I decided you're my future."

"And you're *mine?*" she asked incredulously as if it were an undeserved condemnation. "Did you apply for a job at Charles Schwab? Win a Rhodes scholarship? Lose a rich uncle?"

"Hey, one step at a time."

"Okay, Rollo. For example. Where's the ring?"

It was a very good question. I had already told her I was new at this, so that excuse wouldn't work again. "I thought we'd pick it out, you know, together."

"So I could co-sign for the time payments? A ring is supposed to be two months' salary, Rollo. Now, I'm not saying I'd insist on that, but I'm giving you some perspective here." She paused for emphasis. "You can't afford the prize in a Happy Meal."

"Babe, I got plans."

"Yeah, two rubbers in your pocket," she smoldered. I marveled at her X-ray vision (she was even looking at the right pocket). "My name's not Babe." Was her upper lip breaking into a dew? "And you're clumsy. If we had a baby, you might drop it."

Where does this come from?

I searched my memory for some inexcusable gaffe I'd committed in front of her, but I was at a loss. It was such a silly reason that I began to see her objections as nothing more than anxious denial — a reluctance to confront the intensity of her true feelings for me!

I started toward her, an approach that I meant to end in a comforting embrace. As I said, "Everybody worries, but that never happens," I raised my arms in supplication, swinging the ice-cold bottle of Dom. Its slick, clammy surface defied my grasp. The bottle slipped from my hand and thudded to the floor, connecting with the toe of my right Reebok and inducing a sharp pain and what would eventually become an ugly multicolored bruise.

"Owwwwwwww." Desperate for any affection at this point, I would gratefully accept sympathy. Although the embarrassment hurt more than my foot did, I went for an agonized wince and gave a little hop.

I thought I detected genuine concern. But just then, the doorbell rang, and her expression changed to panic.

"You can't stay," she said, indicating that menace lurked on the other side of the door.

"But we —"

She was conflicted now about whether to answer the door or tend my foot. "Did you think I dressed for you?"

A sense of my own boyish charm returned, perhaps because I was in free fall, with no hope of pulling out. "Well, now," I said, "I didn't think you were taking the dog for a walk."

She didn't have a dog, which suddenly struck me as odd, given the recurring theme of her artwork. It would certainly give us something to talk about next time. I'd invite her for dinner some night, try to find a way to suggest casual dress and modest fare.

She primped before a mirror, straightening a wisp of hair and delicately wiping the delicious sweat from her lip, finishing in a sexy pucker.

"His name is Stan," she said emphatically. "We're going to the opera."

What a droll sense of humor, I thought. It was her deft way of easing my pain without resorting to physical touching, not the choice I would have preferred. "You can't take a dog to the opera," I laughed, appreciating her joke.

I knew a good exit line when I had one, and as she moved toward the door, I grasped the knob and opened it wide.

There stood Stan, the human equivalent of a deep-chested Rotty, with a neck as thick as my waist, draped in an Armani suit that probably cost what I make in a year, shooting an immaculate cuff to expose a glitter on the wrist that was sure to be nothing less than a Patek Phillipe.

I smiled winningly at him, hoping to come across as the innocuous boy next door who had just popped in for a cup of sugar or advice on a gay relationship. "She met you at the gym, right?"

CHAPTER 3
THE GRUEL THICKENS

Wuthering Palms has changed hands more times than a Vegas silver dollar. The current owner is a Dutch conglomerate funded by a coven of VCs. In my parent's generation, that meant Viet Cong, reputed to be vicious, heartless torturers who thought nothing of letting you bleed slowly to the verge of unconsciousness until you gave them exactly what they wanted, then left you for dead. Today's veecees are venture capitalists. Ours grow tulips instead of bamboo, and they have good complexions and smile a lot, but otherwise the old definition still fits.

They grabbed the Palms in a distress sale from some sultan's wife or other, whose hubby was unwise enough to establish California residency long enough to learn the legal definition of community property. A gazillion dollars in handcrafted custom refurbishing and overpriced knickknacks later, our offshore owners put a stop to their own bleeding by cutting back on staff and posting Save the Planet cards in all the bathrooms, encouraging guests to reuse bed linens and towels, a politically correct move that reportedly saved them thirty-two percent on outside laundry bills. Delighted at reinventing the old Dutch concept that less is more, they decided that the new, reserved ambiance should damn well cost more and doubled the rack rate, with not the slightest dip in occupancy. Hype and perceived luxury drive the overheated economy of early twenty-first-century America, and to hell with those old-fashioned notions of value for money.

In a stroke of mismanagement I am still unable to fathom, these bog meisters retained the sitting hotel manager, a Boston Brahmin long past retirement age, one Hugo Farnsworth. A blanched prune done up in tweeds more suited to some musty Victorian drawing-room than the cabanas of Beverly Hills, Farnsworth loathes the public, especially the nouveau-riche techno-youngsters who abjure sensible lodgings at a Hilton for the ersatz splendor of our frilly, pink-stucco bungalows. Maybe that's what Monica's image does for this place. People who stay here must feel they're *in* a Hollywood soap opera. Anyway, Farnsworth is rarely seen outside his fake-book-lined, leather-upholstered office, and some say the trill of his house phone is so soft it won't wake him from a snooze.

THE MORNING after I'd interrupted Felicia on the way to the opera, I limped over to the shop before the start of my shift to pay her a visit. I wasn't sure what I'd say to her, but if she had a customer, maybe I'd catch a stray remark about the mysterious Stan.

On my way in, I noticed the Rolls out front, which did the place no harm imagewise, and I made a mental note to re-park it just as soon as I'd changed into uniform (but not until I'd gotten the scoop from Felicia).

Whom should I find reclining in the beautician's chair but Ms. LaMonica, her face smeared in a mudpack. As if this weren't enough to discourage me, I soon learned that Management was having me followed. I sensed Farnsworth's ghastly hand on my shoulder, transformed into the paw of his familiar spirit and assistant manager,

Hector Gomez-Ibarra. The wicked old fart must have sent him after me because otherwise Hector is one cool dude, maybe even my best friend when he doesn't have a hard-on from reading up on company policy.

He was not in a comradely mood. "Those jalopies don't park themselves, *pendejo*." He apparently thought I'd made a habit of joyriding in the Rolls, when in fact I'd only had it out once (so far).

"Hector, old man," I said as I gave him a playful jab in the shoulder. "Took out the Rolls *yesterday*. Capital. I was thinking of taking the Maser for a spin."

"What-*ever*, Rollo. Just get behind the wheel of something quick or we both gonna be telling bad jokes in the unemployment line."

Never too quick on the uptake, Monica finally stirred from beneath her mudpack. "Who's there?" she demanded imperiously.

(My version of what happened next differs from later third-person reports.)

Hector put on his best hotelier manner, hands clasped as if in prayer (a needlessly stagy effect, I thought, since she couldn't see him). "Miz, er, Jones! I hope we haven't disturbed you? Do you have everything you desire?"

Monica's voice was a low rumble, a jaded growl from the depths of despair as fame faces the monster of rapidly advancing age. She said, "You must be kidding," or words to that effect.

The star's animation put Felicia all a-flutter. "Aye, Miz Jones. Don't talk!" Wetting her hands, she hastened to rework Monica's plaster job. "Your Sedona red clay is going to crack, then I don't know what."

Job done and mired hands upraised like a surgeon, Felicia stormed over to us, clack-clack in those platform shoes that give a provocative rise to her round little rump. "You fellas get lost," she whispered. "I'm getting her life mask, and you almost ruined it. Think of it — I'll have her in clay!"

"She'll have you in court," I said.

"Never mind," said Hector and urged me out the door.

No sooner were we out of the shop than Hector turned on me. "*Qué estúpido!* I catch you once more borrowing vehicles..."

"Fringe benefit," I explained. "*Doit de seigneur, noblesse oblige.* One of those."

He got *muy macho.* "This is what's called a verbal warning, bro. I got to go back to my office now and write out on a goddamn form *in fucking triplicate* that I told you this. Blue copy goes in your personnel jacket, buff to Farnsworth. And I got to fax the white to corporate. Next time it's a written warning, and don't make me explain what I have to do for that."

"Come on, Hector. You my homie."

"You ain't got no homies, you little wad of white trash." No mistaking, his Irish was up, not to be casting aspersions on his dear mother in Veracruz. "I'm up for a promotion, and not you, not nobody is gonna screw it up. I'll be looking for a rosewood briefcase, and you'll be looking for parking spaces or you'll be looking for a job."

"Okay, I just went to ask Monica if she wanted her stretch detailed."

I knew he was upset because he lost control of his verb forms: "You lazy and you a liar, 'cause when you not out joyriding you trying to get in Felicia's coochie. I see the Rolls not parked, I know right where to look for you. Who you kidding, man?"

Surprisingly, at that moment, it was easy to think of Hector as my best, truest friend. He had neatly placed my life goals in two categories — fine automobiles and female companionship, not necessarily in that order. He was wrong, of course. He knew nothing of my other ambitions, but I could see how he and the rest of the world, seeing my actions, might form such a rash conclusion. It was a startling, clarifying moment, and I hugged him.

"Jeez!" he recoiled. "Get into uniform and wipe that silly grin off your face. You loco, you know."

"Okay," I said, "just the jacket. Don't make me wear that stupid little hat."

He glared at me and his lips tightened, showing perfect white teeth set in a rakish snarl. He was Fernando Lamas, Ricardo Montalban, Xavier Cougat in a white tropical suit. "Regulations is regulations," he said, relishing his power.

A few minutes and a trip to the employee locker room later, I was dolled up in my regulation attire, looking, I always thought, not much different from an organ-grinder's trained monkey. The uniform consisted of military-striped trousers and a toreador jacket with gilt epaulets, neatly topped off with a braided pillbox hat.

In my haste to return to my post, I ran straight into the Milwaukee sauerbraten, he being distracted loading his camcorder and she slavering her pasty complexion with SPF-99. I bumped into him, knocking his DV cassette to the floor. (Bet the missus has a little digital in her purse. And knows how to email snaps to her Favorites, maybe even how to surf for porn!) Stooping to retrieve it, he jostled her elbow, causing her to stick her own greasy finger in her eye. Each apparently assuming the other to blame, they set to bickering hellishly until they laid eyes on me, which broke the spell, startled them anew, and got them giggling so hard they drooled.

Having gone from media idol to sideshow novelty in the eyes of the public in a single afternoon's performance, I felt no apology was necessary, tipped my cute cap deferentially in their direction, and headed briskly for the door.

From the other side of the plate glass, an amused Laszlo watched me make my way gingerly through the treacherous mechanism of our recent rapprochement. I hated him for his sniggering look, from which I imagined he was playing back his mental video clip of humping me on the lobby rug.

He drew himself up to his full height and amazingly seemed taller than me as he observed, "Wery becomink, dat hat."

The final straw! I marched over to him and bent down, nose to nose with the one person in the world I hoped I could safely humiliate. "You little Hunkie sausage," I sneered. "Where's your green card?"

He gulped and took one step back. I felt like Attila the Hun.

Ashamed my crisis of self-esteem had forced me into a testosterone standoff with a mild-mannered middle-aged midget, I strode down the walkway to retake my rightful, albeit temporary, place in command of the Rolls.

CHAPTER 4
A FEDERAL CASE

Special Agent Arlen Pugsley here. Excuse me for interrupting an ambitious literary work in progress, but it falls to me to provide some context. Hemphill's painting a picture, so I need to give you the frame. You see, if you've been squaring yourself all along with Uncle Sam, your tax dollars paid for this book. (That won't cut you any slack at Barnes & Noble, I'm afraid. But you've paid for the Internet several times over without so much as a whimper — so what's the point of whining about it?)

I'm a federal parole officer. That puts me somewhere between a bully and a shrink most of the time, and I don't do a bad job. I didn't start out to be some kind of Maxwell Perkins to this snot-nosed Hemphill. But I freely admit I encouraged him — no, I required him — to get his filthy stuff off his chest and onto paper.

Tell you why.

I'm a bit heavier, in terms of seniority and expertise, than your average caseworker. (Yeah, okay, there's my physical heft, too, as long as we're being honest.) Most of the time, my job falls to some junior paper-shuffler who has some training in psych or criminology. But today, your big crimes, your terrorist incidents, and even your wars can be perpetrated and waged with keystrokes and mouse clicks. Unauthorized penetration is the name of the game. So we got an interagency task force for investigating high-tech misbehavior. Includes the Bureau, the warfighters, and the spooks. (Homeland Security fits in there somewhere, but that org chart is way too complicated to explain.) We keep an eye on kids who have too much intelligence and free time, too little ambition and respect for authority, and a talent for cutting capers with computers. Hackers are my specialty, and it's my mission to apply my number twelve shoe to the soft, fat asses of these little pranksters before they get the idea of selling out to some criminal syndicate, corrupt foreign government, or extremist cell.

Fortunately, we got hold of Hemphill before he went rotten. What turns a slacker into a hacker, then a hacker into a hardened felon? In my opinion, the underlying cause is sexual frustration. Masturbation and abuse of computers go hand in hand, is my theory. The perps are mostly young males. They begin to experiment in their early teens. Goes without saying, if they could get laid, they wouldn't feel the need to reach out and touch someone in cyberspace. The Net gives them easy access to porn, chat rooms, webcams — the whole disaster — but for these guys it's mostly one-way, voyeur stuff, choked chickens. A fourteen-year-old with zits who just blew his allowance on another gig of RAM isn't going to make any kind of in-person sexual rendezvous. He's got zero chance of being a real player in that game, and he knows it. Oh, he'll go through the phase of playing the email impostor, but he's no closer to gripping any flesh but his own and soon gets bored. When it dawns on him he can't complete a sexual transaction, he'll turn to the other — the financial kind.

And in that turning, he goes from being a more or less harmless prankster to practicing as a journeyman thief. Now, we can't exactly nip his thing in the bud. If we rounded up everybody who's beating his meat in front of a computer screen, we might as well turn the country into one big jail. But try any funny business with a credit card, and my team is all over your ass.

Hemphill actually didn't draw our attention until what we'd call the second turning — when they start putting their skills to practical use for some client or other. At this point, the perp has gained some proficiency as a hacker. And maybe it's been a few years and the zits are clearing up, so he's got a shot at romance, even if it's a long one. The objective is to impress the prospective girlfriend. Travis Bickle, you get the idea. Certainly, your hacker hasn't spent his teens competing on the playing field or working out at the gym. He's got one trick to show off, so he uses it.

In Hemphill's case, his second turning came at age seventeen. Up to that point, he was pretty much an innocent — literally nickel-and-dime stuff to prove to himself he could pull it off. (We regard even those small transactions as serious. We've had cases where millions were embezzled one penny at a time.) But Hemphill was toying, amusing himself, not racking up big scores, and so he stayed mostly below our radar.

But then he starts to hang with one Audrey Skolnick, a groupie turned pulp-rag stringer. She was a few years older, already out in the world. An aspiring journalist who covered the garage-band beat, that one was a real trash collector. Ordinarily, her work would be no concern of ours (unless she turned political, as some of them do). Problem is, this material girl couldn't balance a checkbook and lived on plastic. She hadn't done it long enough to go bust, but when she took up with Rollo she was several thousand in the hole and sinking fast.

For whatever reason — out of the goodness of his heart, you might say — he offers to go online and help her out. Works some transfers, zeros her accounts, cleans up her credit report — and in so doing pops up like a dummy on our shooting range. That's when we nailed him.

We couldn't get her as an accessory because, according to his testimony, it was all his idea. She didn't encourage him, and if you believe his story, she didn't even know what he was doing until after he'd done it. Said he borrowed her purse when she was sleeping, and that's all it took. We had no way to prove otherwise, so she skated.

He drew three years — six months in a minimum-security facility and the rest on the outside in my tender care. It was a feather-light slap on the wrists, if you ask me, but the guy's got this wounded-puppy look, and maybe the judge bought into that, I don't know. It is hard to believe he could be malicious, but then you've got your Ted Bundy, whom you'd take for a straight arrow from prep school, so there's no telling from appearances.

My job is, see he stays out of trouble and works on his low self-esteem. Bully and shrink, like I said. And it's always the low-self-esteem thing. That's your fallout from your sexual frustration. Did he even score with Audrey, after all that? Damned if I can tell, and he's not telling me. In the pen, he won't so much as pick up a tennis racquet, volunteers to wash pots in the commissary. His only bitch is he wants lotion for the chapping from his hands being in hot suds all day. Which they give him, we're not monsters. But he won't crack a book, won't share in group, won't talk to anyone, and shows his defiance of authority by putting hospital corners on his bunk when they're not required.

He was shaping up to be a hard case, and they were glad to be rid of him. First thing I do, I line him up a good job — no minimum-wage gig, and not washing pots. Parking cars at a classy hotel — Wuthering Palms — with a full forty-hour week, health plan, and 401K. Back in the old days, before this tire showed up around my waist, I used to coach youth basketball at the Police Athletic League. My star player was a guard — would you believe it? — a short brown kid named Hector from Boyle Heights. Played like a terrier. Ends up assistant manager over at the Palms. A phone call did the trick. My boys remember me.

Of course, Hemphill has the skills, if not the formal training, to handle a computer job. But, at least while I'm on the case, we don't want him going near one. Or teaching, for that matter. No warping young minds in ways we can't control. Or maybe even understand.

Which brings me to the task at hand. Hemphill shows no ambition. On the job, he doesn't break the rules particularly and does what he needs to do to get by, but Hector says he's a dreamer. Talks about wanting to be a deejay but doesn't follow through. In our meetings, I bring it up, I get a blank stare, and he changes the subject.

So I suggest maybe he should keep a diary. He doesn't have to show it to me, but maybe some stuff will come up he wants to talk about. He doesn't go for the idea, sees it as make-work, I guess. But a few months later, he changes his mind and tells me he wants to write his "confession." Now I'm all ears. Not only because, for the first time, I'm seeing signs of his being interested in something — but also because both yours truly and my fellow wizards are always eager to let a hacker brag about how he did it. Keeps us current, you might say.

What we got was this piece of shit. Enjoy.

CHAPTER 5
WHOSE LIFE IS IT, ANYWAY?

Despite Hector's warnings, the Rolls was still in my charge. Parked far enough away from the entrance where I didn't think I could be observed easily by my management, the car became my broadcast booth, and, forced to switch brands, I found a discarded bottle of Dasani to use as a prop. Our guests must have been in their rooms rutting or dozing or making it a day at the beach, because no one was pulling out or up to demand my services. So I was free to spin one CD after another. To match my mood, I selected the funkiest, nastiest, meanest blues numbers I could find in my deejay repertoire, which I keep in a backpack as a handy resource for relieving the boredom of downtime on the job.

"This one is 'You're So Mean,' by my main man B. B. King," I intoned expertly into the mic, "who got the lowdown on being looooooow down." Then, a long, deep audible sigh from your host as he exhaled a squadron of demons. "And it's going out to the lovely Felicia. From Dick Head. The one who waits. And throbs."

I was at the top of my form, I thought modestly, although I had no lines lit up with callers eager to commiserate. But I could imagine those millions of appreciative, lonely, misunderstood slackers, who, having wiped out on their dates the night before and being chronically unemployed or taking a sick day on account of heart trouble, had nothing better to do than to sleep in, comforted by the sound of my voice on their radios.

No sooner had the prospect of my conquering the airwaves begun to comfort me than a little Miata pulled up. It was taxicab yellow, a color I'd advised its driver against purchasing. A familiar scrawny figure with a tousle of fuchsia hair popped out. Wearing short-shorts, showing a lot of leg, and powered by a pair of three-inch fuck-me pumps, Audrey clicked saucily toward me.

Not bothering to get out of the Rolls, I pressed a button to roll down the window.

She was chewing gum, not a flattering effect. "Rollo, let me cool you to something," she said as she masticated happily. "When you just drop by? Unannounced? That's not dating. It's called stalking."

So it was clear to me in a flash that Felicia had already phoned Audrey, my ex and her best friend, to report on my recent failure to capture her heart.

"Unannounced? I told her we needed to talk."

"Yeah, well, she was probably thinking it was about the price of haircuts over coffee on her break, you know, not some lame proposal of marriage for chrissake when she's headed out the door on a date with another guy."

"Speaking of Stan, how'd he do?"

She tried to hide her amusement, not wanting to encourage me. "He failed the written test, if you must know. But that doesn't mean you got a shot, understand."

The news that it was a tragic opera even for the unwitting Stan didn't make me feel any better.

One Night Stan — did he get some before the swinging door slammed him in the ass?

Audrey was quirky and sweet and had that rare quality of being enthusiastic about giving head, and I had literally committed crimes for her. But there was no going back, and we both knew it. We never married, but to her that was a technicality. She claimed all the rights and privileges of the woman scorned, although anger never came into it, just a kind of mutual loss of interest. Problem was, she knew way too much about me, and now her best friend was the love of my life.

As she handed me her keys, she said, "You help me out, I'll help you."

Surely she wasn't hinting for me to straighten out her finances again. "You got to be kidding" was all I said.

"I never asked for anything illegal. Just dish me some dirt. You find used rubbers in the back of Monica's stretch, you know who gets the tips." She winked to let me know the salacious pun was intended.

Dirty talk with no hope of physical follow-up was never a turn-on for me, but Audrey fancied herself as a verbal stylist. A tendency to over-cuteness was one of her weaknesses as a journalist that might impede a promising career one day, but I withheld my literary criticism and just nodded. Hotel employees hear it first, and sniffing for the tiniest rotten scraps of celebrity news is what Audrey does. She's truly fond of Felicia, I'm sure, but the beauty shop is the hub of the gossip mill in any civilization, so all the more reason for her undying loyalty and frequent visits.

As I parked the Miata, I wondered what aspects of my performance in any category were being discussed at the moment in Felicia's shop. Little did I suspect a die was being cast that would mold my future.

AUDREY WAS ON A MISSION. She knew that Felicia's star client was one Jayne Jones, and she even knew about Bungalow B but wasn't brazen enough to go there. She preferred the sneaky approach, debriefing Felicia after each of the star's appointments. So far, she'd had to settle for scoops of chickenfeed, but today that would change.

A genuine secret and devoutly desired piece of data was Monica's age. She was not so old as to have lost an allure that once forced rich playboys to endure humiliation willingly, but let's just say that now she probably hoped she looked fortyish on a good day. It was a feat no beauty treatment could achieve without the underpinnings of skilled plastic surgery, and let's just say her state of repair was state-of-the-art.

Now headed for Felicia's shop on leaving me in the Rolls, Audrey was about to learn the backstory of Monica's treatment session of this morning. As I think back, it was then that things must have started getting out of hand, but who knew what bizarre events would flow from a simple slip of the tongue? I eventually learned the following version of Monica's conversation with Felicia — the story Audrey was on her way to hear. It came to me too late, but I've inserted it here, closer to the beginning of my story, to help you make sense of subsequent happenings. If, back then, even after having been so sorely spurned by Felicia, I had known I had any kind of a chance with her, I would not have resorted to the scheme that eventually backfired with such stunning success.

FLASH BACK to that morning in Felicia's place of business at the Palms. I now present an alternate version of the scene previously described. A version with complications. The current episode of *The Edge of Endlessness* is playing on the small portable TV propped on the edge of Felicia's workstand. Monica can only listen as, draped in a plastic drop cloth, she reclines in the chair and Felicia smears her face with a mudpack.

On the screen, Monica is once again making a show of fending off the advances of the ardent Buck. The camera's soft focus, a technique stipulated in her contract, obscures any lingering imperfections as it comes in for a closeup, moving past and then over the shoulder of this guy who wants her so badly he'll try to take her in the boardroom of her media conglomerate in the middle of a typical workday.

"Ohhhhhhh, Buck," Monica's character coos breathlessly. "We shouldn't." And as he caresses her, she elaborates poetically, "Oh, Buck, Buck, Buck!" (At which point, I bet her Teleprompter operator gets out of sync, unable to track a proliferation of bucks the star has thrown in for good dramatic measure.)

In the Palms, under its breath, the mud monster mutters, "Buck, Buck, Buck. They call that writing?" (It's not acting, either, but who cares?)

Felicia, who had turned to the sink to wash up, steps quickly back. "Monica, try not to move your mouth. We're trying a new kind that hardens."

"Waiting for it to get hard, story of my life," the monster muses, chuckling through the muck.

At this point, Hector and I arrive on the scene, not in that order. Then there's a little exchange between him and The Monica I didn't catch.

I'm standing there when he says something like "I just dropped by to see if Miz Jones has everything she needs."

"If I ever get enough, you'll be the first to know, big guy," Monica says with unashamed suggestiveness. *Now, I just don't remember hearing this.* My attentions are elsewhere. But for a heartbeat, Hector is thrown, caught wondering whether he's really being propositioned by a megastar, and he wonders how to respond. His better judgment kicks in, and he realizes she's jerking him off, but not before he audibly swallows hard, giving her the satisfaction of knowing that sex with her is not unthinkable for him. It makes her day, but she doesn't let it show.

As far as Monica is concerned, the encounter is over. Hector's at a loss for words but keeps on grinning like a shameless suck-up, and we're both outta there. (So, I swear I didn't witness what followed. The rest of what transpired in the shop that morning was passed as top-secret information from Felicia to Audrey. Here follows Felicia's version of her transactions with Monica, as recounted to Audrey, as recounted much later to me.)

Apparently, when they're alone and the thing is indeed hard, Felicia pries the life mask carefully from the famous face and sets it gingerly on the workstand.

"What do you intend to do with that?" asks Monica, indicating the stony replica.

"Do you mind if I keep it? I would never sell it or anything. It's just, you're, like, my hero. We should all hope we look so good when we get —"

"My age? How old do I look?"

Oops. To a beautician, this question is the no-win equivalent of "Do I look fat in this dress?"

"Old enough to know better, young enough not to care." A seasoned spin doctor could not have done better. And, hat-tip to Constantin Stanislavsky, whose acting theory has taught generations of scoundrels how to lie with conviction, the line came out as if Felicia had just thought of it, even after a thousand performances.

"I bet you make out on the tips," says Monica as she smiles wisely, one veteran actor catching out another but more than willing to accept flattery under any circumstances.

"Let me keep it and I don't need a tip today," Felicia offers, showing she well understands the mindset of a celebrity accustomed to trading on favors in lieu of cash.

Satisfied the deal is done, Felicia smiles politely and resumes her washing up.

"Is something bothering you, dear?" Monica asks.

"It's fine," Felicia said, not looking back. "Don't worry about the tip."

"What I mean is, something's bothering you," Monica insists. "Is it man trouble or just boy problems?" (A nicely put nuance, and she would know the difference.)

Subtext: *Two can play the gossip game, sweetie.*

When Felicia doesn't reply, Monica figures she's guessed right. "Who is he? Not one of those two..."

Felicia tries to toss it off. "Not the Chicano Welcome Wagon, the other one. He's just a rookie trying to score."

"Damn, I couldn't see. Is he cute?"

"Kind of a fixer-upper," Felicia says, not knowing why she feels it necessary to be honest. (Come to think of it, given the state of my self-esteem at the time, it was a fairly apt description.)

"Does he adore you?"

"I suppose he does."

The phone on the workstand purrs. Felicia excuses herself and picks up. Hearing it's Audrey, she steps out of Monica's hearing. Audrey asks if Monica is still there, Felicia cryptically says yes, Audrey gives her instructions, Felicia hesitates then agrees, and the call is over.

Feeling a loyalty to Audrey that transcends her Beauty School Oath to maintain client confidentiality, Felicia pretends to be rooting around for supplies and opens a drawer. As she reaches in for a handful of cotton balls and a bottle of astringent, she flips on the pocket voice recorder lying there and leaves the drawer open.

"So what about you?" Felicia asks, trying to make it sound like casual, chatty, innocent curiosity.

Monica sits, tweezing a few clinging scraps of clay from her brow. Leaning close and dropping her voice, she says, "Honey, listen to me. There was only one true love in my life, and I almost let it slip away."

Pure fucking gold.

"But Miz LaMonica," Felicia says, for benefit of the recording. "You're not getting married again, are you?" (She could use coaching from Stanislavsky on that one, but apparently Monica is on guard anyway.)

Monica hesitates, then just says, "Never you mind." She tweezes some more clay. "Does this stuff do anything for my skin, or was it all about getting your little souvenir?"

The mask-as-souvenir concept obviously appeals to Monica's vanity, validating her status as one who belongs to the ages (just, not yet).

Felicia decides to press her luck. "So, are you... between boyfriends?"

The star finds this funny. "Between boyfriends. There's a visual. Honey, you can never be too rich, too thin, or too satisfied. You can never get enough. Die wanting more, my motto."

Felicia let the recorder run until Monica left the shop, but the ensuing conversation was just the usual chickenfeed compared to the gold she'd already harvested. And, having been alerted on the phone, Audrey was already on her way to pick it up, which she did, moments after greeting me in the Rolls.

Now you might think learning that Felicia is capable of such deviousness would be a turn-off for me. You might think less of her, but I sure don't. No, I find her loyalty to Audrey totally understandable and entirely forgivable. I'd done as much for her and more — and to this day I'm not sure why. Maybe it's that gossip is fun and conspiracy is great fun? Audrey was one of those kids in grade school who generate subversive ideas and instigate irreverent actions — like putting dog shit on the teacher's chair or gluing the answer key shut. And she rarely got into trouble herself — some hapless follower (like me) would usually take the fall.

Dante's Beatrice may have been the image of perfection, but I didn't want my Felicia that way. The capacity for deceit in a woman gives her an aura of mystery and adventure, or so I thought.

And besides, if she were perfect, she'd want nothing to do with me!

CHAPTER 6
PERSONAL PREFERENCES

Hugo Farnsworth, the Lord High Commander accountable to my Dutch Masters, was a curmudgeon given to dressing as a yachtsman whenever he wasn't in his dour tweeds. He had no use for water other than to splash it in his Glenlivet to soften the bite to his palette and the assault on his delicate and chronically irritable stomach lining. My dealings with the General Manager (GM) were thankfully rare, as he was prone to hiding in the paneled splendor of his office, which was decorated to movie-set perfection, no doubt to either impress or discourage volatile guests who go there to register complaints. There, surrounded by barrel-sized Ming vases, spotless Waterford crystal, and hopelessly cute Lladro figurines, Farnsworth sat like a landlocked admiral behind a Chippendale desk the size of a warship and did who-knows-what all day long.

Actually, I think I know what. Even I am embarrassed to say, but I've vowed not to spare any details here. If I spoon the shit on him and some others, maybe I can get enough of a rhythm going that I'll eventually dig up some on myself. (That fat creep Pugsley has threatened to edit this. Or, cross-reference and hot-link, publish on classified CD to his gang of spooks, and who knows what else. So my other tactic is, throw in enough trash, maybe his Magic Marker will miss a scrap or two. Having trouble with any of the references, Arlen?)

As much as the mass media parade so many varieties of pleasure before us, why is it such a sin when a poor sod actually manages to experience some of it? Life, Liberty, and the Pursuit of Happiness. That last one is a mountainous challenge and a dizzying climb, and, some think, the only reason to get out of (or stay in) bed in the morning. Which brings me back to the apparently harmless peccadilloes of His Excellency the Admiral, the Blanched Prune.

How Farnsworth passed the workday was the subject of active speculation among the staff, but the rumors all converged on his fondness for his cat. Now, I never saw him do anything — er, unusual — and as with my descriptions of other events I could not have seen, I am prone to fantasize and no doubt embellish, stretching a few known facts into a nourishing meal, much as the resourceful Chinese chef can make a few bits of shrimp and diced pork go a long way.

What does accuracy — or even truth for that matter — have to do with a good story?

Time was, Farnsworth had a huge yellow tiger cat he called Lascivia. She was the size and shape of a Swift's Premium Butterball turkey, and about as smart. Everyone reporting to his office was greeted the same way — the slack-jowled old man seated regally behind his enormous desk, Lascivia cradled on his lap, both of them staring at you as if resenting your intrusion on their intimacy. He stroked the thing continually, and if that hand had worn a large signet ring, the effect of an evil genius plotting the end of civilization as we know it would have been complete.

Somehow I got the blame for Lascivia's demise. The dainty thing abjured every litter box set out for her and instead preferred to do her business among the peonies planted just outside the sliding-glass patio door of the executive office. Okay, we all have our preferences, and this was hers, no permanent harm done. Why the GM couldn't make it a responsibility of the groundskeepers to remove the evidence I don't know, but following her around with a beach-toy plastic trowel and a bucket was one of my regular chores.

No one told me I was supposed to be her bodyguard.

So one day when Nero, the house Doberman, came leaping over the bushes, I just thought he was feeling frisky, and my main fear was that he'd tear up the flowerbed. But before I sensed any danger, he had taken the cat in his jaws, lifted its fatty bulk so fast it didn't shriek, and shook it briskly with a snarl, neatly breaking its neck.

Dropping Lascivia's body among the blooms she had loved so dearly in life, Nero looked back at me like a Marine who had just successfully extricated innocent civilians or arguably culpable contractors from a hostage situation, and bounded away. What he had against the cat other than innate interspecies rivalry, I have no idea. (They hardly knew each other.)

I couldn't bring myself to tell Farnsworth right away. In that brief moment, I wasn't even sure what I'd seen. Since Hector was my supervisor, my next move should have been to report the whole incident to him, relying on his knowledge of company policy and his toadying relationship with the old man to resolve what one does with a feline corpse freshly fallen in the flowerbed of a luxury hotel.

But just then, who but Farnsworth should emerge from the sliding door of his office, calling out tenderly for his heart's desire, who best he knew had simply lingered over the posies after a productive but otherwise uneventful visit to the crapper.

There was no preventing his spying the sizable mound of inanimate furry flesh reposing on the damp earth.

From there, he looked straight at me. I felt the blood drain from my face and my skin break out in a clammy, guilty sweat.

Farnsworth had the vacant gaze of a soldier with his arm suddenly shot off, perceiving the loss but not yet feeling the pain. Nero had gotten away clean — there was not so much as a paw print in the moist dirt for me to point to. Time stopped for me then. Good thing I'd already made my own modest deposit for the morning, or

I'd have soiled my uniform. The implications on my career and my personal welfare were beyond my poor powers of immediate calculation. He must have thought I'd killed the love of his life. To me, this was way beyond missing a parole appointment or even getting caught with a firearm. (Arlen, I was never afraid of you!) But this, this was worrisome in the extreme, because I was terrified of Farnsworth even on a good day, and I couldn't begin to imagine what type of cruel and unusual punishment he would devise to fit such a hideous crime.

I've deprived a powerful man of his pussy, perhaps the only pussy he will ever love. How bad is that?

Without a word, he disappeared into his office, gently sliding the glass door shut — too gently. I imagined he was calling the police. I didn't know what to do, so I just stood there. Eventually, it was not he but Hector who emerged from the office, and by that time I had replayed the scene so many times in my head, I was prepared to describe what happened in slow-motion detail. But no explanation was required of me. With a reverential nod to the large kitty's remains, El Chicano Grande handed me a slip of elegant blue writing paper with gilt border and deckled edge. On it was written, in the broad cursive of the GM's prized Mont Blanc, a Burbank street address, curiously lacking the name of any business establishment or resident.

With Lascivia slipped into nothing grander than a Mobil Hefty drawstring garbage bag, I dutifully drove to the specified location.

It was a taxidermist.

Weeks later, I did not call for the processed version of Lascivia when it was ready. Evidently insured shipping or private messenger or some other type of secret conveyance had been arranged. Although I had kept my mission and its destination confidential to this point, I fully expected the cat would be out of the bag eventually, perhaps reappearing on the set in the role of an incredibly lifelike plush toy. (I've seen those in stores, so why not?)

But the eerie glass eyes of a furry replica were nowhere to be seen.

Rumor was, Lascivia had become a pelt. One could easily imagine her as a throw rug in Farnsworth's private bath, but a reliable source (not for the record: Hector) reported seeing a limp, golden paw dangling from the hastily closed top right drawer of the admiral's Chippendale. So, to phrase it concisely, the conclusion is inescapable.

Farnsworth is still stroking that pussy in private.

Only now she doesn't take bathroom breaks and incurs no veterinary bills other than an occasional freshening with Goddard's Dry Clean Spot Remover.

On the morning after I'd made an even bigger fool of myself at Felicia's, the admiral summoned me to the bridge. Hesitating outside the door to Farnsworth's office, I was met by Hector, whose concurrent arrival meant he'd been paged for the same meeting. My compadre did not look pleased.

"No need to be paranoid," he said. Then, as he swung the heavy oak door open, he muttered, "He really *is* out to get you."

Confucius say, career of ass-licking leave bad taste in mouth.

It was clear from Hector's expression that he wasn't about to protect me this time.

Farnsworth wore a double-breasted navy-blue blazer and a pair of white ducks, topped off with a foppishly tied ascot. Although traces of cat hair would be easy to spot on the dark serge, I didn't see any. And there were no traces of animal parts protruding from any of the desk's myriad cubbyholes. Presumably, he had planned for this meeting and prepared.

After an overture of throat-clearing, he began, "Hemphill, about this joyriding in guest vehicles..."

"We were parked," I blurted.

"*We?*" Farnsworth and Hector spoke at once.

"All right, I was daydreaming. But she was only a dream, okay?"

Farnsworth ignored my explanation, apparently assuming I'd been under full sail (actually pressing the old gal into service instead of languishing in her) when apprehended. "My God, the liability," he said. "Do you know what they charge for a touch-up on a Rolls?"

Does he want a price quote? Am I supposed to know the answer?

"Why," he went on, "for a chip the size of your fingernail they sand and they polish, sand and polish, *rub, rub, rub* — repaint the whole frigging body — then, if it's the slightest bit off, a sag here or a pucker there, they remix and redo the bloody enormous thing. Oops, here's a bit of a ding, and they start all over again, *rub*bing and *rub* —"

He began to wheeze as he worked himself into a state of breathless anxiety. Hector went quickly to him and covered his mouth with a paper donut sack (which must have held this morning's petit-fours).

The wheezing subsided, and what passed for calm returned to the sea.

"End of story, don't let it happen again," Hector said to me, as if reading lines intended for Farnsworth. Then to the old man he confided, "You fire him, I got to get day labor, and my Spanish ain't that good."

Farnsworth growled like a lion who'd just missed snacking on a gazelle. "I've got my eye on you, Hemphill," and indeed I thought I saw it twitch.

He rose ominously, then announced, "We have a new, very special, long-term guest, Mister Hemphill. One Jayne Jones, Bungalow B."

"Monica LaMonica, everybody knows. Old news." I said, turning to share the joke with Hector, who wasn't having any.

From his look, the admiral was about to go thermonuclear. "*B* for *be discreet,* you pathetic little dweeb." Throat clearing. Jacket straightening. A brushing of the lapels. "See that her every miniscule wish is abundantly fulfilled, won't you?"

He studied me as if inspecting one of his nameless starched swabbies, then complained to Hector as if I'd left the room, "He's out of uniform."

"Oh, no. Not the hat," I said.

OF ALL THE things you can set on a grown man's head, nothing will reduce him more effectively in status — nor devastate what little might be left of his self-esteem — like a pillbox hat. The cuter and smaller, the better for the penis-shrinkage effect, and mine was scarcely larger than the missing cap on one of my Evian bottle-mics.

The hat punishment came with the job, just one irksome aspect of the devil I knew. But I suspected the humiliating pain of it was chump change in comparison to the wealth of hurt Farnsworth surely had in store for me.

CHAPTER 7
FBI SIDEBAR

Pugsley here, in my role as Max Perkins. (On second thought, make that *Marlon* Perkins — ha! — what a zoo.)

Now, my pet perp's mewling confessional is pathetic, no question. But you salt it with some independent corroboration, supplement it with third-person data gathered in the field, and just maybe it starts to look like some kind of meaningful case study. *Lessons learned* is the new management buzzword when there's plenty of blame to go around, and I've got to do my job.

I'll try to be brief and relevant, resisting the understandable impulse to editorialize and sticking to the reports I have on file.

Case in point, many of Hemphill's conversations in and around the location of the Wuthering Palms Hotel were not only observed but were also recorded by cooperative witnesses.

The senior couple he disparages and then dismisses so cavalierly in the preceding narrative turned out to be one Lucille Honeypacker, white female age seventy-two, and her husband Woodrow ("Woody"), a white male age sixty-nine, both hailing, not from Milwaukee as the smartass surmised, but in fact from some wide place in the road you never heard of just outside Benton Harbor, Michigan.

The Honeypackers belong to that modestly affluent class of transient Social Security suckers who hurtle down the nation's highways toward their last sunset in big tin cans on radial tires. Dedicated star-stalkers, they piloted their custom-outfitted Winnebago to the Left Coast and implemented their own amateur surveillance program, possibly in hopes of sweetening their pensions by selling clandestine video clips to the media. Having ingeniously equipped their vehicle with audiovisual gear for the purpose of electronically hunting some Big Game, they closed in on their apparent target, whom it took them no time to discover was resting in the Palms under the assumed name of Miss Jayne Jones, Bungalow B.

You see, Lucille thinks Ms. LaMonica is just the cat's pajamas. And Woody, who pretends to humor and enable his wife in an innocent hobby, has had a secret hard-on for the star for longer than most of her fans have been alive.

I was nosing around the Palms myself, monitoring Rollo on the sly, when I got wind of the Honeypackers. In the normal course of events, the Bureau wouldn't give them a second look — none of their trespasses necessarily rise to the level of federal crime. Invasion of privacy and stalking are state offenses, and parking illegally and living aboard a motor home on the public right of way in Beverly Hills usually get no more than a yawn and a misdemeanor citation from the local cops.

But when I began to appreciate the evidentiary potential of the recordings, not to mention their value as supplementary literary material, I introduced myself, flashed the badge, debriefed the old folks, and later subpoenaed their videotapes, from which I hoped to gain insight on Hemphill's motivations, activities, and modus operandi. (I'm fortunate to have a working knowledge of digital moviemaking from an extension course I took. You can't work in this town without brushing up against the Industry now and again. I even had a screenplay nearly done about a terrorist plot in an airport, but some sleaze-ball bastard I pitched it to in a taxi ripped it off and I don't have a thin dime to show for it. You probably saw it, and now you know.)

Perhaps most revealing of the early tapes, labeled "OGLING THE CARHOP" with a bold Sharpie, was made when the liveaboards were parked just the other side of the tall hedge that separates the circular drive of the hotel from a wide, tree-lined stretch of Sunset Boulevard. From this hidden vantage point, the camcorder's telephoto lens caught Rollo behind the wheel of a parked Rolls Royce, apparently oblivious to the world as he slacked off, engaged in one of his elaborate Mittyesque fantasies.

(Technical note: Woody had cleverly mounted a hypercardioid shotgun microphone to the camera. This type of mic focuses in on sound much as a long lens will grab a tight shot over the same distance, making it possible to get a reasonably good rendition of picture and sound in the areas of the driveway and the main hotel entrance from, let's say, fifty yards away.)

On the morning in question, Hemphill had donned a pair of wraparound sunglasses to top off the playboy look he'd attempted with his thrift-shop blazer and slacks. The tape shows him alternately pretending to steer the vehicle and then waving expansively to an imaginary crowd. From this and information I gleaned in our parole sessions, I surmise that these fantasies typically adhere to a set of themes, most of them built around movie motifs. This one (his favorite apart from his manic deejay rants) places him in a street scene of Fellini's *La Dolce Vita* as the dashing Marcello Mastroianni, who, parodying himself as the womanizing leading man, is hotly adored on the screen as in life by a female peasant class in the rural postwar villages of his homeland, where the glitterati in Rome were and still are worshipped as gods.

In the passenger seat beside Rollo, I'm guessing, he pictures his fantasy version of Felicia Ferrulo, whose nice little figure would make Anita Ekberg flush with jealousy. (Okay, I said I wouldn't editorialize, but take it from me as a trained observer, she's a looker!)

As he waves, we hear Rollo's falsetto on the soundtrack:

"Ciao, Rollo! Rollo mio! Oooooo, Rollo, molto sexy!"

As the scene rolls on, the Honeypackers' voices intrude on the track, sending the camcorder's automatic audio gain circuit crazy as it tries to compensate for their nearness, making them sound uncomfortably loud as their carping echoes off the walls of the enclosed trailer. (Technical note: Amateurs should learn to turn the AGC off to prevent this problem, which the pros suggestively call "pumping.")

As Woody played videographer, Lucille scoped the scene with a pair of Bausch & Lomb high-powered field glasses.

"That little pecker is one sad case," she says, adding her own caption to the scene.

The framing of Rollo's antics jiggles as Woody tires from holding the camera through the long stakeout. "Next time, what say we switch off?" we can hear him say. "You work this thing for once and I get the glasses."

"Nothing doing," she says. "Who saved up the Piggly Wiggly points? You got the camera and the camp stove, as I recall."

"*She* could walk by any minute," he grumbles, recalling Lucille to their mission of stalking celebrity quarry. "And here you go ogling some car jockey."

"Woodrow, a young man should get his gun off now and then. I don't see there's much hope for this one."

"You got no business thinking them things about him. It's not him we come all this way for, not by a long shot."

She then interjects some personal innuendo to which I guess her husband was unusually sensitive (not an uncommon dynamic of disagreement in long-standing relationships, I've found): "You know, if we'd've let Junior get lucky once in a while..."

The camera angle goes way off and loses focus as Woody lets it drop and turns all his attention to her. But before he kills the power, the audio has his terse reply, "Oh, now *I'm* the bad parent?"

THERE FOLLOWS a timecode break on the tape, possibly indicating he'd had the time to rewind and replay the clip before resuming. What we see (and hear) then is Hemphill's conversation with Hector, my protégé and his supervisor, on the occasion of Rollo's decision to go forward with yet another of his dubious schemes. This one was a corker, and it gave rise to the world of hurt that followed.

CHAPTER 8
A PLOT LAID AND HATCHED

Adored by thousands of cheering fans who lined our route, Felicia and I were motoring through the narrow streets of Rome on our way to a date with the paparazzi at Cinecittà when Hector strolled over to the car and rudely leaned into the shot.

"You don't learn, do you?"

It was in the heat of a weekday afternoon, and a respectable stillness had descended over the Palms. Our guests were either trying on yet another $400 pair in the air-conditioned lap of the Saks shoe department, or they were alternately napping and rutting in their sumptuous suites. I therefore saw no need to take his rebuke seriously.

"Some pal you turned out to be," I pouted.

As I expected, his tough look evaporated, and the sniggering smile of Hector my homie took its place. "You take the heat, the old man lets off steam, everybody got a job," he explained. His expression broadened to a 100-Watt Aquadent smile. "No worries. I got your back, bro."

"Why doesn't that make me feel all cuddly, I wonder?"

"Don't fuck up this job," he said. "Or maybe you want me to

sponsor you for dishwasher at Barney's Beanery, something like that?"

He'd more than made his point, but I didn't have to acknowledge it because at that moment a familiar white stretch Town Car pulled into the drive.

"Battle stations," I muttered, getting out to resume my post at the curb. Hector noticed I hobbled a bit.

"You get anything off Felicia last night?"

"When she realizes how perfect we are for each other..."

"Just what I thought. Nada," he laughed as he jerked off in pantomime. "She stomp your foot?" He obviously already had too much information. Felicia doesn't speak to him (she thinks he's a wannabe gigolo), and Audrey confides nothing without getting large gossip currency in return. So I wondered how much he knew about my aborted proposal, and from whom.

"I'm getting ready to make my move and some guy named Stan shows up. Built like a refrigerator, wearing this majorly hock-able gold watch. How does a normal guy compete with that?"

"Gotta make her jealous," Hector said, his gaze tracking the limo's approach. (Among the words that will live in infamy, those are surely some, planted by my compadre at that moment like virulent seeds in my fertile unconscious, there to proliferate like some nasty weed until all my thoughts, waking and otherwise, would be focused on that single goal.)

With Hector close behind (following through on his promise to watch my back) I was in motion toward the rear door of the car, but her driver Ernie Washington was way ahead of me, making a show of earning his salary.

"Miz LaMonica!" Hector was the first to exclaim as she jumped out at us. On this hot day, she looked like a giant snowball dressed all in white fur, gorgeous gams at one end, an explosion of fiery red hair at the other.

As Ernie quickly grabbed her shopping bags (Gucci and Halston), her trademark heart-shaped shades swung around to focus on him

— training the killing power of her 10,000-gigawatt estrogen laser on him.

"I'm seventeen minutes late for my pedicure, Mister Afraid-to-Change-Lanes."

Ernie gulped, there being no defensive posture against such deadly force.

Always the diplomat, Hector edged toward her. "Is there anything — ?"

She grabbed the bags from Ernie and shoved them at our always-helpful assistant manager. "Here, put these in my bungalow."

At this, Ernie's timidity modulated to full-out panic as he must have wondered whether he'd be fired on the spot, deprived of the menial task of schlepping the spoils of the hunt to her beastly lair.

"Traffic was a b —" he started to say, as if in apology.

Error! Miscalculation! The laser's twin lenses swung back on him in a flash, locking him in her sights.

"I hear the b-word from you one more time and they won't let you drive a golf ball. On a public course."

Amazingly, that was the only firing she would do, this time.

Removing her lenses, she turned to me. In my role as bystander, I must have represented the millions of her sympathetic fans. "You see these?" she asked, removing her lenses and pointing to her eye. Her face came close and I got a strong whiff of Passion. "Type-A worry lines. There isn't enough mud on the planet to get rid of these!"

Ohmigod. What could be worse than an all-out estrogen laser attack? We three knew — it would be every man's worst nightmare: a storm of tears, which would rain down like thermonuclear ash, entombing our hideously charred bodies with their shriveled penises until the next Flood. For reasons no less noble than saving every healthy dick on the planet, I prayed she would show restraint.

Hector — how does he manage it? — bent and scraped even lower. "Perhaps the lady would prefer to slip in by way of our rear entrance?"

She went right to the core of his meaning, however unintended.

Tensions evaporated, she laughed, then gibed to me, "Go figure, a man who asks first."

She flounced off rat-tat-tat in her ruby-red alligator heels in the direction of the deserted pool patio (a shortcut to Felicia's shop). Ernie heaved a soulful sigh of relief and shot us a commiserating look as he climbed back into the stretch and drove off.

Hector handed me the shopping bags, then reached into his pocket for a key-access card.

"Why don't you drop these over to Bunghole B," he smirked, "seeing as how's you and her are new best friends."

I studied the card. "Is this a passkey for the whole damn hotel?"

Replacing the smirk, he did a very convincing menacing glare. "*Pendejo,* I'll know if you steal so much as a Cheeto from the minibar."

CHAPTER 9
TAKING ACTION

On my way to Monica's bungalow to drop off her purchases, I mulled over Hector's suggestion: "Gotta make her jealous." By giving me the bags to deliver along with a wink and a passkey, was he thinking that I'd pop 'round to the star's suite and offer whatever services she might require? Perhaps he didn't appreciate how intimidated I was by her and how lacking in confidence that I could fully satisfy, much less simply fulfill, her desires. Just getting it up with all those gigawatts trained on me would be challenging enough. But then I'd have to be not only effective, but also diligent, enduring, and probably also creative in ways I couldn't even imagine.

I want to imagine. If I only could!

If I could become a more imaginative lover, wouldn't I be more attractive to Felicia? They say it's more fun to learn than teach. If I had no hope of ever having her, shouldn't I learn how to love whatever comes?

As my brain reeled with fantasies of burying my nose in a mound of red hair, my heart was elsewhere. I felt more like one of Felicia's adoring big-eyed puppies. I wanted no one else but her. And if that meant eating out of her hand and learning to fetch and carry, that was fine by me. Naive as it sounds, I truly wanted to be her friend first, then see where that took us. True, I had tried to rush things the other night, but that's what I thought she expected. I know women complain about guys who make passes, but aren't they just as upset when the guy they're interested in can't even make the first move? (Like a putz, I just assumed she was interested. Maybe she was, is, could be. I had to hope.)

Make her jealous. He has something there.

So as I approached Monica's suite and rejected the idea of coming onto her (before I even had the opportunity), it dawned on me that, to arouse Felicia's jealousy, I didn't really have to *do* anything. I just had to make her *think* that I did.

And if Hector thought Monica and I were a possibility, why couldn't Felicia?

～

I ASSUMED Monica was getting her overdue pedicure from Felicia at that moment, so on the off chance that Monica was thinking what Hector was thinking, I was thinking it would be wise to leave the bags sometime when she was out of the room — like now.

But as I passed the side window of Bungalow B on my way to its front door, I heard voices coming from inside. I lingered in the shadow of a convenient shrub and listened.

"So what are you saying?" The man was angry.

"You're a fine specimen," Monica said, "in the prime of life. You're fit, you're strong. You could easily find another job."

Ernie! So maybe she had stopped in on her way to the shop, and he came by to jack up his job performance? Or, he confronted her outside and she dragged him in here to avoid a public scene.

"So you're firing me after all?" he asked. I wondered if she wasn't hitting on him. He could be in trouble no matter which way it went.

She took a while to reply. "No, but I have to watch the pennies.

You'll have to be satisfied with what you're getting now. I don't know how long I have."

"To live?!" If Ernie were her lover, which I figured was a possibility judging from his familiar tone with her, it would be doubly cruel that he wouldn't get his raise because she would soon need expensive cancer therapy.

"On the *show*," she said. (This certainly sounded like a scene from *The Edge of Endlessness*.) "My contract is pay or play. They could kill me off at any time, even mid-season. All I want, all I ever wanted, was *one more season*. But sooner or later, it'll be *Kill the Tigress*."

"You're saving for your retirement?"

"I hate that word," she said. "It's 'seclusion.'"

Ernie sighed and said, "If there's nothing else..." and pulled the door shut with a petulant slam on his way out. He passed me on the garden path and saw me carrying the booty from Rodeo Drive.

"Sorry to keep you waiting," he said and stalked away. In the two months since Monica had installed herself at the hotel, he and I hadn't had much to say to each other. In that moment, I was sure he saw me as an eavesdropper and a cowardly suckup, guilty as charged.

No need to use the passkey. She responded right away to my knock, probably thinking it was Ernie coming back and wanting the last word.

"You take the long way around?" she asked, taking the bags but not wanting an answer or offering a tip. She closed the door firmly in my face.

So much for resisting temptation — there was none to resist. I held a snapshot of her in my mind, standing there in the doorway in a Chinese silk dressing gown, her hair done up in a scarf. There was not a hint, not the tiniest muscle twitch, of sexual innuendo in that stony face. Who was I kidding? Any rumors about Monica and me would have no credibility. Unless... I needed some kind of visible demonstration. I needed to put on a show.

CHAPTER 10
WITH LUCILLE AND WOODY

That afternoon when Hemphill intended to deliver the goods to Ms. LaMonica and was spurned just as quickly, the Honeypackers had her bungalow staked out. Woody did some nice handheld camerawork (really, pretty respectable).

Here's what the video shows (not much audio from that distance): Rollo marches up, ducks under the window, overhears who knows what, Washington comes out, they exchange a brief greeting, Rollo delivers the bags, walks away, no big whoop.

As night descended, there was no visible activity in that part of the hotel grounds, no lights came on in the star's unit, and the Honeypackers concluded that she had retired early. They took a break for a quick repast at Souplantation, then resumed their positions in the shrubbery. The bungalow looked just the same, and they were satisfied that not much had transpired during their brief dinner break.

The bungalow has a light on the porch and another above its private garden patio, but both were switched off. To shield guests from the annoying glare of security lighting, the only other illumination on the interior grounds of the hotel is provided by Malibu lights lining the pathways between the detached units. (From the viewpoint of security, it's a substandard situation, but we're talking celebrity sensibilities here, so who gives a rip about my expert opinion as a lifetime law enforcement professional?)

So the area around Bungalow B was shadowy, providing perfect cover for Lucille and Woody and, they would soon learn, for a mysterious Someone Else.

Along about 8 P.M., Lucille was alerted by a footfall on the path, and she told Woody to switch on his camcorder. (He was smart to activate its low-light function, but even then all he captured was a blurred form.)

So we can't rely totally on the tape as evidentiary matter, but combined with testimony from Lucille, whose night vision was considerably better than Woody's electronic view, we have a fair description of the intruder's disguise, if not his appearance.

At first, she was sure she was watching OJ Simpson, and she had to stifle a gasp.

Putting it all together, we know it was an adult individual of medium height, wearing an extra-large trench coat that made me suspect he was heavyset, disguised by one of those celebrity rubber Halloween masks made to look like the retired NFL player / sportscaster / movie star. (The famous case was old news even then, but it makes you wonder whether the intruder had some sick sense of humor, some agenda besides just hiding his face.)

He hesitated on the path to the bungalow, just a few feet from Lucille's position in the bushes. She saw the mask animated hideously by the anxious panting of its wearer, as the slobbery mass swelled and slacked with each labored breath. (Can we assume the guy was stressed?)

He turned stealthily as if checking his surroundings before making his next move. Fortunately for the sake of the record, he didn't spot the Honeypackers. She told me she was concerned for Monica's safety, naturally, but at the time she couldn't think how to alert anyone without putting herself and Woody at risk. (But if you ask me, they knew they were onto something and decided to stay put.)

As the intruder sneaked up to the bungalow, Lucille followed as closely as she could without revealing herself by stepping into the lit pathway.

Rather than knocking or using the buzzer, he did a kind of mouse-scratching, very subtle-like, on the door with his fingernails.

Faint as the sound was, the lights in the unit came on right away, the door opened, and he slipped inside.

Now suspecting they were tracking a tryst in progress, the Honeypackers moved to the side of the unit, where the window was ajar, permitting Woody no good angle from which to get video, but offering a gap large enough for him to slip a lavaliere microphone and cord through. He connected it to the camcorder and thereby managed to capture the conversation inside.

During this time, Hemphill had been skulking about. Although his shift had ended some hours before, he seemed to be fascinated with the goings-on in Bungalow B. He happened by moments after Woody Honeypacker had planted his bug. And, hiding outside the window, he must have eavesdropped on pretty much everything we hear on Woody's audio.

What we hear on the tape is a muffled, hideous chuckle, followed by a frantic tussle. But no screams, no audible protest.

That is, not until, after a minute or so, Monica exclaims, "Uggggggggggh." But not as though she felt threatened. More like she got a sip of soured milk or a mouthful of bad clam.

At last she said clearly in an exasperated tone, "Oh, Merl. Take off that rubber thing."

"Oh, yeah." It's the only thing we hear him say, and it doesn't make much of a voiceprint. I played it back dozens of times and couldn't figure out whether that husky quality was normal or a growl of passion. (So much for audio forensics, and I have all the latest software.)

After that, footsteps retreated into another room and the lights went out. The Honeypackers waited all night, even tried dozing in alternate shifts, but — go figure, amateurs! — they missed seeing the guy come out.

After the tape came to my attention, my follow-up check of the hotel security log and inspection of tapes from its security cameras turned up nothing.

And no complaints from Monica. At least, not about *that* incident.

So the guy got away clean. But the Honeypackers had a clue. Or thought they did.

Merl.

CHAPTER 11
GETTING A HEAD

My fantasies having been all but extinguished by the ice-water reception I got from Monica, I started to lope back to my post in front of the Palms. It was nearing the end of my shift, and I looked forward to turning my duties over to Laszlo. (Although to call him "my relief" was going a bit far.)

Scanning the vehicles in the parking lot on my return, I observed that Audrey's was gone, leading me to conclude that she'd harvested what news she could from Felicia and driven off to slave over a hot laptop. (My fate awaited the appearance of the next issue of *Loose Lips*.)

With Audrey gone and Monica's pedicure probably not happening, the thought occurred that Felicia was probably gone for the day. She usually closes her shop in the late afternoon, after her last appointment.

Having no customers myself and being bored but not stiff, I shoved my hands in my pockets, there to reconnect with Hector's plastic passkey.

A devilish thought: Felicia's shop was empty, and I had the means to unlock any door in the hotel.

I don't know where the idea came from, or even what I intended to do exactly. It was probably some primitive, reptilian panty-sniffing impulse, but the prospect of breaking into Felicia's shop and rooting around in her business was indescribably delicious.

When that runt Laszlo showed up, all uniformed, spit-shined, and wearing his little cap proudly, I briefed him on a Mustang in the fold and an Excursion in the field and trotted happily away.

Arriving at Felicia's shop door unseen, swiping the card to trigger the electronic deadbolt, and slipping inside were way too easy.

The place was dark and smelled like a spilled bottle of Clairol.

I swear at that point I had no plan. I was a private eye rummaging through my shifty client's desk looking for some damning clue. I was a scum-loving bottom-feeder looking for a morsel of edible detritus. I was a rabid movie fan looking for some titillating scrap I could cherish as a souvenir for the rest of my natural life.

Then I saw it. *The head.*

I was startled at first. There on a shelf by the workstand, the dark silhouette of a bald, decapitated Monica stared placidly out the window at the evening sky. Spooky, let me tell you. When you see that kind of thing in the half-light, your brain kicks into survival mode, and you have to pinch yourself to realize it's nothing to be afraid of. (Or maybe it was, if I'd've known better.)

There was a towel on the shelf beside it, as though Felicia had tried to cover the ghastly thing with all due respect. She must have unveiled it for Audrey, then perhaps not thought to replace the shroud as she chattered on excitedly about the coup of copping a life mask from the world's greatest living soap star.

Also nearby lay a pair of Monica's trademark heart-shaped sunglasses. I noticed one of the lenses was cracked. Maybe since they were broken she'd gifted them to Felicia to go with the head and start a collection of star-crap memorabilia. Monica probably buys them by the case, so why bother getting a broken pair fixed?

I don't know which I had first — the impulse to steal the head or the knowledge of what I could do with it — but I stole it. I wrapped it in the towel and carried it off in a plastic bag I found in the trash. I almost forgot the glasses, then dropped them in, too.

I was so eager to have my prize that I didn't think much about whether I'd be suspected of the theft. As far as Felicia knew, Hector was a tease, he had seen the mask, and he had a passkey. And for sure she'd shown it to Audrey, who had more than enough reason to sneak in later and make off with it.

On the way home, I realized what I could do with it. There's no harm in joyriding with a dummy, as long as you don't try cutting into the diamond lane. And the trick would be innocent enough. Felicia wouldn't even have to see us, as long as *somebody* at the hotel did and the rumor mill got hold of the story.

THE NEXT DAY I called in sick. On hearing the news, Hector sounded almost relieved, and I wondered why but didn't bother to ask.

Now, for me, taking a sick day requires a monstrous amount of courage. Oh, I don't care at all what they think of me at work, or even whether they dock me or think I'm a slacker. (I *am* a slacker.) No, my fear is having to live with, deal with, just muster the will to simply look at my apartment in the daylight. I rent in an industrial district of Hollywood that's full of sound stages, studio equipment rental warehouses, taco stands, custom welding shops, liquor stores, and adult novelty shops. But it's not my building's dingy exterior or my garage-sale-eclectic decor that gets me down. It's having to deal with my own waste matter. The square footage that people euphemistically call my living room is littered with old Domino's Pizza boxes, grease-soaked KFC cartons, Chin-Chin carry-out containers, Subway wrappers, several empty tubs of Ben and Jerry's Cherry Garcia, and a small truckload of empty Coors tallboy cans.

There are probably bugs, but they hide from the daylight, so that's the good news.

I'm torn between a perfectly respectable desire to throw the mess out and a twisted fascination with the bright colors it lends to the otherwise drab, gray walls. I can't afford art except for a few rock posters from the resale shop, but my collection of commercial food packaging looks like an Andy Warhol installation that the tortured artist wrecked in a fit of self-loathing. The overall impression almost works, when you view it that way and don't dwell on it too long.

(Another thing I haven't got is a computer. Even if they let me have one, I wouldn't. Everybody's happier that way, believe me.)

First thing that morning, I ran my errands, starting with a Starbucks Espresso Roast Grande (the cup added a much-needed touch of green to Mt. Trashmore). And I stopped at the art supply, where I picked up a pint of liquid latex, a broad bristle brush, a camel-hair detail brush, rubber cement, and some tubes of acrylic paint. Then I popped into the adult novelty shop, where I paid cash and tried to adopt an indifferent expression as I bought an inflatable life-sized rubber sex toy. Other purchases that morning included a Styrofoam wig form, a bright-red full-length ladies wig (synthetic, of course — who could afford real?), a used raincoat from the Salvation Army, and a fancy-looking but cheap scarf with a woodland motif I hoped could pass for a Hermes.

The total damage was $159.63, ironically about what I might have spent on a bottle of fine champagne to achieve the same result.

Arranging the art materials on my kitchen counter, I laid the wig form facing up. I unwrapped the clay mask from the towel and, taking care not to damage it, set it gently on the form. Monica stared blankly up at me, just as no doubt she had assumed the same position for countless dermatologists, beauticians, depilatory technicians, dentists and oral hygienists, studio makeup artists — and lovers.

Dipping the bristle brush in the liquid latex, I slathered the mask with five successive coats, carefully letting each coat dry before applying the next. Painting the lips made me hard, and I tried to think of how many heavy-metal bass players I could name.

As the final coat was drying, I squeezed acrylic paint in a variety of colors from tubes onto a dinner plate. Enjoying getting funky with my fingers, I mixed the colors literally by hand. That was the most difficult part. I tried to match the skin tone on the back of my hand, figuring that would be close enough. But getting a color that wasn't too white or too pink or too brown wasn't easy. Eventually, I got frustrated and started a new plate. (When the paint dried, rather than wash them, I'd add both to my art installation.)

After maybe an hour of mixing and getting nothing but sick-looking skin tones, I had one that didn't look too bad, and I painted the latex face all over. Figuring I didn't have to worry about detailing the eyes because I had her sunglasses, I concentrated on using a fine brush to apply red lips and some artful (I thought) shading to the nostrils and laugh lines. Doing the lips made me hard again, so I really concentrated on the nostrils, which were interesting but not lust-provoking.

I got increasingly excited as the rubber face acquired living color, but I had to take a deep, calming breath before the next step, which was delicate and tricky. Of course, I still had plenty of liquid latex, and if I damaged my work in pulling it off the clay form, I could start over. But there was something about the skin-like quality of the face, despite its rubbery composition, that inspired in me a kind of reverence and professional care. I felt like one of Monica's trusted plastic surgeons as I peeled off her skin, rolling it slowly and gently away from the red-clay skull. I was careful, and the latex and its coating of paint must have been sufficiently dried and cured because the fake skin didn't tear.

I balled my fist, placed the rubber skin over it, and held it up to the light, admiring the result. Using Felicia's clay mask as a mold, I'd created a lifelike rubber replica of Monica's face.

Figuring I'd be all the more clever if I could secretly return the clay head to its rightful owner, I wrapped it in the towel and returned it to the plastic bag. I set the wig form upright on the counter and draped my new latex version over it. Monica looked out, her makeup looking realistic but for a pair of vacant eyes, and I could almost hear her say, "You've got your nerve bringing me to this dump."

Imagining I was hearing her effigy speak could become an annoying and possibly unhealthy habit, I feared. If she started offering advice, I resolved then and there to pay no attention.

I left her in the kitchen to take in the ambiance and perhaps come up with some redecorating ideas. (If she was going to have opinions, at least they should be useful.)

Brushing aside the remnants of Warhol's fit from the sofa, I sat and took the rubber doll from its box. I unfolded the instructions, and I was surprised to see that the directives refer not to the setup procedure, which is assumed to be simple and self-evident, but to varieties of usage and performance with the full-figured doll. So the instruction sheet reads like a script for a porno movie. A no-cost extra!

I found the inflation stem located, appropriately enough, at the belly button. I was in the process of giving it (her?) lungfuls of air — and turning my face red with all the blowing and panting — when there was a knock on my door.

I guess I'd left the door ajar, because Hector just walked in. He took one look at what I was doing and said, "I always wondered what you did in your spare time."

Instead of bothering to reply, I just kept on blowing.

Sitting down next to me, he picked up the instruction sheet I'd thrown on the floor. "'Guaranteed lifelike or your money back,'" he read. His eyes grew wider as they scanned the page, and he let out a whistle. "They got an 800 number here for product support. Eh, there's a job."

I stopped blowing. "Do I need to find another job?" I asked.

"Maybe," he muttered. "Look, I shouldn't have razzed you about Felicia. I'm getting no coochie myself just now, but this is sick, man."

Couldn't he guess what I was up to? "You said I should make her jealous."

"Not like this! Aye, what you're gonna do is against my religion."

I pinched off the doll's umbilical cord with one hand, reached over, and handed him one of my shopping bags.

He pulled out the trench coat, the scarf, and the heart-shaped sunglasses, then took a moment for it all to sink in.

"Don't even think about it," he said, looking very worried.

BUT HE MUST HAVE BEEN curious, because he stayed and even helped. A half-hour later, we'd rubber-cemented the latex face to the inflated doll's head, dressed her in the raincoat and scarf, sat her in a chair, and topped her off with the wig. Hector applied the finishing touch as he fitted the sunglasses to the bridge of her nose.

As he played Igor to my Dr. Frankenstein, we stepped back and studied our creation, our admiration tempered with scientific detachment.

I didn't think she looked all that bad, figuring the effect at a hundred yards was all that mattered anyway.

"There is something about the hair," I said.

Hector looked at me like I was in full denial. "The hair? You kidding? You gotta take in the whole effect. You're no Michelangelo."

"What do you mean?"

No sooner had I asked than I detected a new lack of enthusiasm from the Creature. She must have had a pinpoint leak somewhere because she was starting to slump, as though she, too, was less than thrilled about her looks. As her head lost fullness, her face started to crumple. The wig went askew, as did the sunglasses, which, being cracked, weren't helping the illusion anyway.

No doubt about it, she was losing her pleasing plumpness, slowly transforming from a voluptuous starlet into an elderly invalid before our very eyes. Within just minutes, it was sadly apparent that no one would ever mistake her for a real human being — at any distance.

Her end was not pretty.

Oh, we had the technology to rebuild her, but what about the reliability factor? Her shoulders simply weren't strong enough to bear the weight of our mission.

Hector sighed, "Get your money back, man." He moved toward the door and, turning back, asked, "You still got the head?"

I went into the kitchen, grabbed the sack that held the toweled bundle, and, amazed at my daring but seeing it was the right thing to do, handed it over to him — along with the passkey.

He quickly strode over to the doll, plucked the sunglasses from her face, and tossed them in the bag.

On his way out, brandishing the passkey, he said, "I'm gonna cover for you one last time. You get your sorry butt over there tomorrow morning, no shit Sherlock." Then he added, "Monica's doing a war dance about something in the papers this morning. You better hope it don't involve you, or it's *adios* for always, my friend."

When he'd gone, frustrated in achieving my goal, I was restless and confused. I filled a dozen trash bags with food cartons and disposed of them in several trips outside to the dumpster. It didn't take nearly long enough, and afterward the place looked naked and shabby. My only consolation was the thought of disappointing all those cockroaches who would show up soon after sunset for the Early Bird.

In that moment, it was just me and my rubber friend, alone in a humorless void that had no past and no future.

It was a foreshadowing of things to come.

CHAPTER 12
A HOT STAR GOES SUPERNOVA

According to Hector, no sooner had he left my place with the stolen property than he got a page on his cell, summoning him to Farnsworth's office.

There stood Monica, dressed in day jewelry and Chanel ensemble as though her next stop were a ladies' tea in Bel Air. She was fuming. In her hand was that morning's edition of *Loose Lips,* which bore the headline: "MONICA'S SECRET LOVER!"

Farnsworth had been manfully accepting a tongue-lashing on his own, and when Hector arrived, she was eager to do them both.

"I won't live in a goddamn goldfish bowl," she growled.

"Miz LaMonica —" Hector began.

Wielding the paper as though both of them were clueless about the accusations it contained (which they were), she continued, "They've got me practically married again. Next thing you know, they'll be making all kinds of irresponsible —"

Clearing his throat importantly, Farnsworth intoned, "Miz... Jones. A star of your magnitude, a woman of your celebrated beauty — is it any wonder the public is curious about your love life?"

"Listen to this crap," she fussed, as she found a passage and read,

"Miz LaMonica confided, 'My only love, I almost let him get away. Now I'll never get enough.' End quote. Never get enough! What kind of slut do they think I am?"

Hector and Farnsworth exchanged looks, both praying the question was rhetorical.

Monica knew that the tabloid quote attributed to her contained a germ of truth, and she remembered the innocent aside she'd shared with Felicia two days ago in the shop. But evidently Felicia was the first person she'd confronted after seeing the paper, even before presenting her case to The Admiral.

Apparently, Felicia had stonewalled beautifully, telling Monica simply that she hadn't said anything to anybody, which may have been technically true, since she didn't mention the existence of a recording or handing it over to Audrey. And perhaps because of the life mask idea and the glasses and all the sucking up, Monica truly believed that Felicia was a loyal fan — a true believer, maybe even a devout worshipper, but surely not a guileless gossip. The Female Mafia has a special subparagraph in its code of silence for psychiatrists and beauticians, and Monica, a Made Woman if ever there was one, could not believe a faithful soldierette would rat her out.

What's more, the Audrey-Felicia connection was known to Hector, but not to Farnsworth or Monica. Hector knew if he disclosed the connection, Felicia's denial would count for nothing and he'd get the gruesome task of firing her. But since Felicia was one of the principal caregivers in the employ of the hotel with a proven ability to Make Monica Happy, Hector was obviously reluctant to dispense with her valuable services. (Maybe he also figured she'd eventually warm to him and he could get lucky, but of course he didn't include that in his report to me.)

Despite the scarcity of likely suspects, Monica still wanted somebody's head, even though she professed no interest in getting her own back. (Who knows, maybe she harbored the hope Felicia was an agent for the wax museum?)

Turning to Hector, Monica asked, "So who else was in her shop the day before yesterday?" The logistics of any third party actually overhearing her confidence to Felicia were physically impossible without the audio recording, but Monica was determined to find a suitable culprit, however flawed her detective work.

"Well, there was me," Hector smiled sheepishly.

For the briefest moment, Monica stared into his eyes and entertained the idea that he was the house mole. But the notion just flitted by, probably because Hector was so well invested in his role as shameless suckup that she knew serious betrayal from him was unthinkable.

She thought back, tapping her chin with a brightly lacquered nail.

"What about her wussy little carhop?"

It was one of those cartoon moments. A big light bulb went off over Farnsworth's head as he detected a familiar source of trouble, and his eyes became slits.

The fact that I'd committed crimes for Audrey Skolnick, girl reporter, was a matter of public record. And payback was overdue for slacking off on duty, flouting the dress code, and, he strongly suspected, killing his kitty.

"Rol-lo Hemphill," he said, as his slow burn morphed into a sadistic, satisfied smile.

CHAPTER 13

SURVEILLANCE PRODUCT

On the afternoon of Hemphill's termination from the employ of Meister Partners PLC dba Wuthering Palms Hotel, the Honeypackers surreptitiously taped assistant manager Hector Gomez-Ibarra in close conversation with Ernest Washington, Ms. LaMonica's driver. Unfortunately for our purposes, Woody did not have time to plant a mic, and there is no audio.

Accosting Washington after he parked her Lincoln Town Car in the lot, Gomez-Ibarra says something that appears to irritate the man, who launches into a tirade. His anger doesn't appear to be directed at the assistant manager, however, because he points repeatedly in the direction of Bungalow B. (Lucille thought he acted like a slighted lover, but Woody opined that he behaved more like an underappreciated employee.)

Hearing the driver out, Gomez-Ibarra permits Washington a peek at the contents of a plastic bag he is carrying. Washington seems puzzled at first, then, paying close attention to the other man's proposal, breaks into a broad grin.

The two share a hearty laugh, and the transaction concludes as

Gomez-Ibarra throws a comradely arm around Washington followed by an enthusiastic handshake and playful shoulder jabs.

Fascinated with anything having to do with the star and aware that Hemphill had been fired, but not knowing the reasons why, the Honeypackers assumed that the assistant manager was trying to make amends for some complaint from Monica about inadequate service.

In fact, as we learned much later, the two had conceived an elaborate practical joke at Rollo's expense.

CHAPTER 14
DOWN THE RABBIT HOLE

I went back to the Palms a week later to turn in my uniform and collect my last paycheck. You'd think Farnsworth would have relished firing me himself, but he'd simply had Hector call me at home. I hadn't shown my face around there until that day, and I didn't even bother to dress up. The best I could manage was a rock-band T-shirt and a pair of faded jeans. I wasn't the least bit depressed, although I can't say I'd done anything productive, much less actually looked for another job. But since I'd had plenty of time to clean my apartment and even do a wash, at least my clothes didn't stink.

As, pay envelope in hand, I walked back to my battered VW Rabbit in the lot, Felicia followed me out.

"They gave you the axe, I heard," she said.

I tried to make light of it. "I no longer wear the uniform, sports fans."

"That's so unfair," she said as she took me aside, checking to make sure the coast was clear. "I'm the one who told Audrey about Monica. She's got a boyfriend, I'm sure of it. It was just such a juicy piece of news. Who knew they'd do this to you? I have to tell Farnsworth —"

I loved her all the more for this sincere expression of integrity and courage, almost as much as I did for ratting on Monica in the first place.

"No, Felicia," I said and saw my chance to embrace her.

"Don't," she said, pushing me away, but gently. "I'm sorry for you is all. Don't get any ideas." Then, "Do you know what Hector did to my head?"

"Aw, he teases everybody," I said.

"The *mask,* you bonehead. The clay mask I made of Monica."

"You know, come to think of it, if Farnsworth found out, he'd fire you for that, and I'd still be out of a job. So no use spilling your guts."

"I know Hector took it," she said. "With that guy, it's always some prank."

"If Hector took it, he did it to tease you about it," I said, not wishing to confess my complicity in the matter. "So just wait him out." Then, I just kind of slipped in, "You still seeing Stan?"

"No," she said quietly.

Who shows up then but Audrey, all purring the way Lascivia used to do when she had a bellyful of English sparrow.

"A reporter knows she's scored when the star gets pissed," she smirked. "And girl, lemme tellya, she is royally pissed."

"It got Rollo fired," Felicia said plaintively, as though Audrey hadn't yet heard the news. "Monica thinks he's the one who gave you the tip."

Audrey laughed it off. "She loves the attention. If she weren't the center of the known universe, she'd curl up and die. She'll settle down eventually, and you can get your sucky job back, although I don't know why you wouldn't use this chance to move on, you know? There must be one or two clubs in Hollywood that could use a trash-mouth deejay."

I let that go, seeing Monica's stretch easing its way into the drive. "Uh-oh," I said. "Looks like we're caught in her tractor beam."

The limo pulled right up next to us, and the driver's window slid down with an ominous electric whir.

"Rollo," Ernie said, stony-faced.

"Ernie," I said, at a loss for a more clever greeting.

Nodding to indicate the back seat, he commanded, "Get in."

"This is a goof, right?" was all I could think to ask. Hadn't I had enough grief over this?

He just stared at me, his jaw set as though it were taking all his effort to be patient.

I shrugged and said confidentially to the girls, "Looks like I get to apologize in person. Both of you are going to owe me for this."

As I walked around to the passenger door, I could hear Audrey say, "What do you suppose she...?"

"She's going to kill him," Felicia said, so seriously it freaked me out.

Audrey wondered, "You don't think...?"

Raising her voice, Felicia called to me, "If she doesn't kill you, you're *dead*, hear me?"

As I opened the door, there was Monica, sitting stiffly as far as possible on the other side, as if afraid of catching some disease from me.

Smiling weakly, I climbed in, trying to avoid the death ray emanating from those heart-shaped shades.

As we pulled out of the drive, Ernie looked straight ahead, offering not the slightest courtesy of further introduction or explanation.

We rode in silence for a few long moments.

Okay, I was going to have to start the conversation. Better to get it over with.

"Miz LaMonica," I started, but I had nowhere to go.

She continued to regard me coldly, and I marveled at how cruelly effective it was of her to hold that intimidating pose and say absolutely nothing.

I had resolved to cover for Felicia, if it came to that.

Finally, I blurted out, "You know how a person will hear something and maybe repeat it, somebody else picks it up, and if it gets repeated enough times...?"

I wasn't getting through to her. I could see no crack in the ice, although, looking over at her briefly, I realized she was wearing the cracked lenses, and I shuddered at Hector's double betrayal of me. He'd not only returned the head and the glasses to her and not to Felicia, but he'd probably also told her the whole story of the rubber doll just to amuse her and clear himself. And here she was wearing them brazenly, yet another way of taunting me silently for my sins.

"I'm sorry. I'm really, really sorry" was all I could think to say.

Nothing but unforgiving silence.

As the limo pulled back into the drive at the Palms, I realized we'd taken a long turn around the block.

Hector was waiting for us at the curb, Laszlo standing officiously at his side. Felicia and Audrey were nowhere in sight, but I guess they'd seen enough. As the car came to a stop, the little man sprang to open the door on Monica's side.

Apparently unmoved by my apology, she didn't move.

Hector nudged Laszlo aside and leaned in to speak with her.

"Miz LaMonica," he cooed, "I hope you took a big piece of this gringo's ass."

Hector leaned in further to address me. Laszlo was jockeying for position behind him, trying to see what was going on inside.

"What the hell did you say to her?" Hector asked me accusingly.

"I tried to apologize, but —"

"Never mind," he said huffily, I assumed for her benefit. "I just want to know..."

He turned to her and — suddenly, rudely, lustfully — he grabbed both of her breasts in his big hands, cackling, "Are these gazoombahs *real?*" He finished by slavering her noncompliant mouth with a messy French kiss.

I about had a heart attack. But as Hector stepped back, it was Monica who sagged over, falling into my lap.

She was stiff as a board — some kind of mannequin — but, unlike my inflatable version, impressively real.

Hector and Ernie were laughing so hard they cried.

Laszlo, who apparently wasn't in on the joke, looked in with abject horror as he squeaked pathetically, "Oh mine God, dey've kilt her!"

A HALF-HOUR LATER, propped up in my threadbare La-Z-Boy at home was the life-sized replica of Monica LaMonica, this one made of flesh-like silicone with a steel skeleton and masterfully articulated joints. With the sunglasses now removed, I could see that the face was an incredible likeness — except for her fixed, glassy stare.

Hector had not, in fact, returned the head to its owner. He'd shipped it to the model maker.

By now, I'd caught my breath and joined in the spirit of the thing. Hector, Ernie, and I popped the tops in unison on our tallboys, spewing brew into the air. The Three Musketeers of Men's Liberation, we clinked our cans in a hearty toast.

"To RealDoll dot com!" Hector exclaimed.

"Beautiful, just beautiful," Ernie said. "They did an incredible job with the face."

"It's amazing," I said, still marveling at the lengths they'd gone to. "I had no clue. What'd she cost?"

"More than I got," Hector said. "And a premium for rush service. I put it on my Visa. You better get a good job now, so you can work it off, my man." He paused and let out a resounding belch. "Well, was it worth it?"

"I guess you guys enjoyed yourselves," I said, still embarrassed at how they'd pulled me in.

"No, Rollo," Hector said. "The look on your face was the icing. The cake was Felicia. We did it, bro. We burned her sweet ass. She probably thinks you're doing The Monica right now."

"You think?" I wondered. My new reputation, if I had one, would take some getting used to.

"Absolutely," Ernie said.

We all took a long, greedy pull on our beers.

"You're a genius, Hector," Ernie went on.

"Hey," Hector said. "It was Rollo's idea. I just ran with it."

It was all starting to come together for me. "The jealousy angle," I marveled out loud. "Farnsworth goes and cans me. Now I got jealousy *and* sympathy. Double score!"

Hector laughed, "Yeah, you got no job and a girl who thinks you're screwing somebody else. Worked out real good."

"No, it's gonna be fine," I said. "And Audrey showed up. Per-fect. They'll have all kinds of stories. You know, in my wildest dreams, I was hoping it'd start some kinda crazy rumor."

"Monica's pretty mad," Ernie said soberly, and he would know. "And when this thing gets back to her, I mean, I got my issues, but still..."

"Yeah," Hector said. "This thing could get way out of control."

I tipped my can to the doll, the queen of my fake desire. She stared out benevolently on her loyal subjects.

"I hope it does!" I said, stupidly.

CHAPTER 15
CRUISING ON SUNSET

Figuring I might as well be hanged for a sheep as for a lamb, I took Pseudo Monica (the P.M., as I came to call her) as my constant companion. I couldn't have squired her in style if it weren't for Hector's collusion, but now that I wasn't an employee, he really didn't care how much trouble I got into. And even though he professed to disapprove of my borrowing guest vehicles for short spins, he was perfectly happy to enable a masterful ruse that he'd prided himself on instigating. He even found me some designer clothes that fit me rakishly, left over from a guest who'd departed unexpectedly when the narcotics squad began to take an interest in his sideline business.

So it was that one sunny afternoon a charity function at the hotel caused Jay Leno, its guest host, to leave his Buick Roadmaster convertible with me for safekeeping.

"Don't sweat it, Hector," I said into my cell phone as my gorgeous rubber friend and I pulled out of the drive. "Nobody's told *him* I don't work there anymore."

The function was set to go on for a good three hours, so she and I had plenty of time to regale our fans on the boulevard.

Monica was resplendent in sports clothes and a long silk scarf that trailed in the wind behind her billowing cascade of fiery hair.

Enjoying this more than any of my previous fantasies while motoring, I gestured to hand her the phone.

"He wants to have a word with you," I told her.

Despite the fact that the sun was warming her silicone skin, she replied with stone-cold silence.

"Sorry, man," I said into the phone, trying to keep up the act and resist a fit of the giggles. "She's in one of her moods. Ciao."

There was always the chance that Mr. Leno would eat a bad shrimp and urgently want his car back early, so after only twenty minutes or so, I hung a right on La Cienega, a left on Fountain, then a left on Sweetzer to double back to Sunset, returning to the hotel the way we'd come.

As I pulled into the drive, I caught sight of Laszlo standing in the middle of the pavement waving his arms. Granted, the car was his responsibility officially, but I thought it was particularly offensive for him to be so impatient for my return, especially when I'd been considerate enough to come back early.

I realized too late that he was waving me off.

As we neared the curb, a swarm of paparazzi — including Audrey — sprang from out of nowhere, aiming cameras with long telephoto lenses.

Audrey exclaimed, "It's them!" mostly for dramatic effect, since they were all in motion already.

I gunned it, and we swept past them so closely I could hear a barrage of shutter clicks like kitten-soft machine-gun fire.

"Whoooooooaaaaaaaa, ambush!" I exclaimed, swerving expertly as a bodyguard-driver averting a terrorist attack.

As the big old car jackknifed out of the drive, I cast a glance back over my shoulder.

Felicia was standing apart from the others, watching the whole thing. I caught her expression in the wink of an eye, and what I saw there wasn't a jealous rage, but simple and sad disappointment.

I raised Hector on the cell. "Did you know about this?"

He said he didn't.

"Yes," I agreed with him. "I would say things have very much gotten out of hand."

Through a short cellular negotiation, he arranged for Laszlo to drive my Rabbit to a rendezvous nearby, where we exchanged cars. When I drove my drop-dead escort back to my own place in my own car, I'm sure no one noticed. On arriving at my apartment building, I slung her over my shoulder and carried her inside. If anyone bothered to report the bizarre sight to the cops, I never heard about it.

Which should tell you something about my neighborhood.

CHAPTER 16
UNINTENDED JEALOUSY, A TRANSCRIPT

Displaying the resourcefulness of a seasoned operative, Woody had left the lavaliere microphone jammed in the windowsill of Monica's bungalow. All it took for him to go wireless was a quick trip to Radio Shack and some imaginative rigging to hide the small black-box transmitter in a nearby oleander. By dint of his diligence, we have the following transcript of a conversation in the suite, recorded as an audio track on his camcorder.

The tape begins with the sound of Monica's Jacuzzi. From the context of his remarks, we can assume that Merl was not in the tub with her, probably standing in or around the door to the bathroom, and we believe he's looking at a fresh copy of *Loose Lips,* the cover of which featured a blurred telephoto shot of Monica and Rollo in a convertible.

"Just who is this creep?" Merl asks indignantly.

"Keep your voice down," she says.

"Answer the question."

We hear her get out of the tub.

"He's a carhop here," she explains, adding, "or was."

"Did he take you for a *spin?*"

"Don't be ridiculous," she says.

"Then who in blazes is this?" he asks, no doubt confronting her with evidence she's already seen.

"A celebrity impersonator, of course," she sniffs.

He wants to stay on the offensive but isn't sure how. All he can come up with is, "Well?"

She fires back at him, "Well?" implying she has nothing to be ashamed of.

"Well, what are you going to do about it?"

"Nothing," she says proudly.

He takes a while to ponder this.

"*Nothing?* Why, if you don't come right out and deny it, the whole world is going to think this two-bit car jockey is doing you!"

Monica's voice drops, and we had to crank up the gain to make out what she says: "You are tenacious, and I like that in a lover."

There's a gap at this point, and we can assume they are embracing.

Then she coos, "You won't have to worry about being seen here if I'm supposed to be somewhere else."

He entertains the thought, then says, "That's like... a license to steal!"

"Now are you coming aboard," she asks, "or am I flying solo?"

There's no dialogue for quite a long time after that.

CHAPTER 17
REPORTING TO THE BRIDGE, AGAIN

The morning the Buick photos appeared in the tabloids, Hector put in an urgent call to me at home and summoned me once again to Farnsworth's office. At first I thought it might be some HR thing, then I worried Pugsley had learned of my termination and perhaps wanted to hear my side in front of them before frying my ass. Not eager to find out but not wishing to piss anyone off any more than I had already, I threw on my new duds, combed my hair, and presented myself as requested.

I was surprised to see the tension gone from Farnsworth's face. The old man looked positively rosy, sporting a new silk suit with a mortician's carnation in the lapel.

A copy of *Loose Lips* was spread out on the desk in front of him.

Indicating the paper, he gave it a wave of the hand, as if dismissing a trifle. "Rollo," he said congenially. "You don't owe me any explanation. After all," and I thought I detected his smile grow broader, "you're not on my payroll." No doubt aware of the laws against joyriding, he mumbled, "Police matter, I suppose."

"Mister Farnsworth —" I began, but he raised a cautionary hand.

"No *need*," he insisted.

I was eager to show him that on careful inspection, the closeup of Pseudo Monica had a certain zombie quality that, I was prepared to contend, betrayed her existence as a fake. Reaching for the paper, I said, "It's not what you think —" and in so doing knocked over his pitcher of iced drinking water, which emptied into his lap. In a flash of horror, I could imagine the wetness creeping into his boxer shorts, chilling his withered balls, creeping up his crusty crack, pooling in the padding of his leather seat.

My karma with this man really sucks.

But he flinched only slightly, trying not to move so as to retain his gentlemanly composure at all cost, although he had to be uncomfortable.

"I don't wish to know" was all he said.

"Mr. Farnsworth, sir," Hector interjected. "Rollo didn't —"

"Señor Gomez-Ibarra y Jimenez," Farnsworth pronounced with an expert Castilian lisp, "I'd like a private word with my friend Rollo."

Hector did a fearful, commiserating take to me, perhaps wondering whether I was about to be caned. Farnsworth rose regally, straightening his wet trousers. I got really worried. As the old man came slowly around the desk, he started to raise his hand to me.

"I'm sooooo sorry," I pleaded, hoping my sincerity could encompass my multitude of sins.

But in a comradely gesture, Farnsworth rested his hand gently on my shoulder and smiled at me collegially.

Hector saw his chance and quickly left the room.

With the slightest nudge, his expression somber now, Farnsworth edged me toward the door. I flashed on Sean Penn in *Dead Man Walking*.

When we arrived at the doorway, he said reassuringly, in reference exactly to what I'm not sure, "It's nothing, truly. How's the foot? Mending nicely, are we?"

In a new tone he must have meant as father-to-son, he said,

"Rollo, my boy. I'm upset we had that little misunderstanding. But of course, I can't permit you to be seen around here. Not as a carhop."

As what, then — a stuffed trophy like your disappeared cat?

"You know," he mused, retrieving a mental picture from the cobwebs of his memory bank, "in my time, I used to like a little... joyride."

It appalled me to realize he wasn't talking about adventures in motoring. Then he shook my hand!

"I'm sure you can appreciate," he said staunchly, "it just won't *do* to have you parking cars. I sincerely hope, however, you'll consider staying on as our... guest?"

I was, needless to say, speechless. In a hushed, conspiratorial tone, he added, "Why don't you drop 'round to her bungalow?"

And with steely seriousness and an arch of his aristocratic eyebrow: "Give her anything she wants."

CHAPTER 18
I GET TO SEE MONICA'S CODICILS

As Hector's trusted lieutenant and now as Farnsworth's conscript, I had been dispatched for the second time to Monica's place of residence on the expectation that she might wish to press my privates into her service.

I found her in the secluded garden of her bungalow seated under a big shade umbrella at a tea table. She was dressed all Laura Ashley with a gauzy dress, wide satin sash, and big, floppy sun hat. And, of course, the heart-shaped shades.

She was reading the second-most-infamous copy of *Loose Lips*, the one with me and the doll on the cover as we rode in the Lenomobile.

She didn't look up as I approached.

"You, ah, sent for me?" I asked.

No response.

"If you want your car, I'll go get Ernie..." I tried.

It seemed forever before she said, without looking up, "Sit."

I pointed to the companion chair at her table.

"Here?"

"It's a new invention called a chair," she said. "Please."

I sat. There followed a long, uncomfortable pause as she appeared to scrutinize every jot and tittle of the tabloid.

"You, ah, got plenty of towels?" was all I could think to ask, just to break the silence, and naming one thing I could actually do something about, however unofficially.

She seemed to notice me for the first time.

"Can I get you something?" she asked. Then, with an appraising glance, "Shirley Temple? Virgin Mary?"

"No. No. Thanks, no," I said, then, considering the height of the hedge and the fact that she could disembowel me without fear of witnesses, I said, "This bungalow is certainly... private."

"Yes," she cooed. "I value my privacy." (She said it Brit-style, so it sounded like *privvy*.) "Everyone at the hotel is so careful." Then, glaring at me pointedly: "*Almost* everyone."

Now, from my undetected eavesdropping, I knew she was having it off. Some guy named Merl. Maybe I didn't get the whole picture, but I got enough.

Does she guess that I know?

Simply and dramatically, she folded the paper and placed it on the table, indicating her readiness to talk. All I could do was stare at the cover photo, reflect on how colossally stupid I had been to think I could get away with such a thing, and wonder what manner of humiliation would come next.

She looked into my eyes, perhaps revising her appraisal of my callowness, and said, "Apparently, everyone on Earth thinks you're 'doing' me." She smiled pleasantly, as if the job required little more than redecorating her suite.

I gulped, "Really?"

"Clever," she said, indicating the photo in the newspaper. "One of my impersonators?"

At least this was a topic I knew something about. "Uh, a doll, actually," I said.

From the sudden change in her expression, this offended her more than she was willing to admit.

"Oh?" was all she could say. "I... had no idea."

I eagerly offered details: "Silicone flesh, steel skeleton, articulated joints..."

The mental image appalled her. "You go in for that sort of thing?"

"Oh, no," I hastened to add. "You see, I was just trying to make someone jealous." Then, realizing she might take this personally, I amended, "Not you."

"Good," she said. "Because I'm not the least bit jealous, I assure you." Cold stare. She picked up the paper, turned to the story on the inside, and searched it, as if looking for some detail. "Mister [reading] Hemphill? What do you want?"

I was taken aback. I was not prepared. Who was she to ask such a thing? Who was I not to have an answer?

"Ma'am?"

"Do you want to be a, I don't know, a studio executive?"

I didn't know that was even an option. I had to think fast. Finally, I stated boldly, "I want to be a deejay."

I was surprised to see it did not strike her as a particularly outrageous request. Without a change of expression, she asked, "MTV? Alternative webcast...?"

Whew, she was going pretty fast. Lemme think. "Drive-time talk," I said, finally. "Top forty."

"Of course," she said. (I guess I'd given an acceptable answer?)

"Rollo," she continued, "you're a resourceful, ambitious young man. I believe you and I can have a mutually beneficial arrangement."

From beneath the paper, she found a formally prepared, legal-sized document and shoved it across the table at me.

"This is a binding employment contract," she explained. "Your job is to guarantee my privacy." (Again with the Brit-talk.)

She leaned closer, then added softly, "And if you ever breathe a word about my private life... well, see paragraph nineteen sub two."

Having no idea what the particulars were, but fairly sure that no other big-name star was about to offer me any deal at all any time soon, I signed. Three copies. One for me, one for her, one for her lawyers. Her *lawyers! Plural!*

Before she could change her mind, I left with my copy in hand, repairing to the Pistachio Bar at the Palms, where, for the first time, I was looking forward to ordering a drink as an honored guest.

Forget that it was not yet 11 A.M. I wasn't sure whether to toast my success or drown my sorrows, but either way, Jack Daniels and I were in for a long, full, and frank exchange of views.

CHAPTER 19
HOLY SHIT!

Still dressed in the Continental duds Hector had so beneficently provided for me, I sat by myself on a stool in the Pistachio Bar and sipped a double sour mash on the rocks. I had signed a tab for my room, which Gracie, the bartender (whom I knew to talk to) had told me was Room 1098 according to the computer — I hadn't yet been there. But I was grateful the account could serve as a resource for purchasing an unlimited number of drinks at the bar.

I was downing my third, maybe my fourth.

It had been an unrealistic day.

I was reading my contract for the third time.

I didn't quite understand the negative consequences specified in Paragraph Nineteen Sub Two, but they sounded dire enough.

Gracie hovered nearby. Until today, I had been her peer, and in a pillbox hat, certainly not one to inspire her respect. But without any prompting from me, she now knew I was a Celebrity Guest Numero Uno. Her attitude toward me had changed to be downright deferential — and this would take some getting used to.

She asked me whether I wanted another, and I said yes, I'm not driving, and I tried to smile. She somehow knew I wasn't driving — would, in fact, simply take the elevator home — and she poured a generous double shot without hesitation.

And she got the joke, bless her — but there was some distance in her look.

Before I slipped into alcoholic delirium, I vowed to stop at the front desk and pick up the access card for my room. I was curious what manner of accommodations the Blanched Prune had arranged for me. For all I knew, it was in the basement, next to the boiler.

I tossed another one back and became aware of the broadcast that was showing on the telly above the bar.

The set was tuned to the news — live coverage of a midday celebrity lunch and media opportunity. A speaker at the podium was saying, "And now, to share with us her vision of a new and vibrant Los Angeles, I give to you, Councilwoman... Merle Cantwell!"

Merle — where have I heard that name before?

This Merle strode to the podium, there to silence the cheering crowd. She was a striking woman, the kind they call "handsome." If she were mayor, she'd inspire respect. And fear.

She spoke: "Thank you, Mack. And thank you, International Brotherhood of Electrical Workers!"

That voice. The name. It was a fit. I could not fucking believe it.

I called to Gracie and beckoned her attention to the screen.

Merl. *Merle!*

But "I can't believe it," was all I said — as I began to appreciate the implications of Paragraph Nineteen Sub Two.

Holy shit!

Gracie shrugged me off, knowing that some guys who drink are fascinated by anything that moves on a TV (which explains why so many bar sets are tuned to bowling or golf).

On the screen, Merle Cantwell was embracing her extremely homely husband Dennis, who waved meekly, clad in a cardigan and chinos. Beside them on the dais stood their pizza-faced son Marvin, who was wishing he could be anyplace else.

Merle said, jubilantly, "Now, I want to thank this fine, progressive union. And I want y'all to think about getting behind the idea of a woman's right to choose — whether she can be *mayor of this great city!*"

Wild, stomping cheers.

Holy shit.

I gulped down what was left of my fourth bourbon. Gracie was right there with the bottle, ready to pour another.

"Believe what?" she asked, innocently.

Lamely, I said, "Councilwoman Cantwell is... married."

"Good for her," she said. "Another shot?"

I fished out a wad of cash to tip her (knowing bartenders prefer the green), but she stopped me, indicating the running tab for the room, which was already lying facedown on the bar.

"Boss says your money's no good here, big guy," she said.

"You better leave the bottle," I said.

I knocked the next one back, the ice banging me on the lip and the nose. "Holy shit," was all I could say, as I watched Merle Cantwell thank the cheering crowd and realized that me, myself, and I were now legally obligated to cover her high-society ass anytime she wanted to be in the sack with The Monica.

CHAPTER 20
I CAN'T TELL FELICIA

I walked into the beauty shop, overdue for my fix, casting lustful looks at my sexy Sicilian. Felicia was busily straightening her workstation after a long day of fighting the war against crow's feet. As she bent over the sink, the way she held her gorgeous legs so straight, ankles primly pressed together in her high heels, and the pleasing roundness of her rump made me think of a vintage Vargas drawing. (I had to imagine the head turned back and the coy, alluring smile, but it was easy enough.)

I was feeling no pain from being at the bar, I had a bad case of the hots for her, and my better judgment had been totally liquidated two drinks ago.

"You get your job back?" Felicia asked, noting my cavalier attitude.

"Not exactly," I said, trying to smile. I weaved a little, hoping she didn't notice. It crossed my mind that if I got close enough to kiss her, she'd smell the booze on my breath, but if it got that far maybe she'd think my lips tasted like candy.

"Was Farnsworth hard on you?" she asked. She sounded

genuinely sympathetic, and I should have taken my chance right there.

"I'm... going to stay at the hotel for a while," I said. "Just until I get a few things worked out."

She looked puzzled. "What do you mean *stay?* As a *guest?* I thought you —" She thought some more about it, then continued, "What's up with this? If you squared it with Monica and Farnsworth, how come *I've* still got a job? Somebody has to get the blame for pissing her off."

It was way too complicated to explain, not that it could ever make sense to her.

I made a pass — at least, *I* thought it was a pass. But our radar must have been on different frequencies. She stepped aside and I missed the target, puckering on air. As I tried to recover my composure along with my balance, she gave no indication she knew she'd been under attack.

"Listen," I said, trying to sound cool. "I'll call you later. I'm going to be, ah, tied up for a while."

Felicia did not take this the right way. "You're *her* little lap dog!" she smoldered. "Did you give her a little *head?* Where's my mask?"

I wanted to tell her everything, and maybe I should've, right then. (Maybe none of the rest of this would have been necessary.)

"You're not going to believe what happened..." I began.

"Oh, no, by all means," she fumed. "Let's be honest. I'll start. I thought you were cute. God help me, I even thought you were, I dunno, shy in your own way. *I wanted to like you, Rollo."*

She looked at me long and hard.

"Women have been doing it for centuries," she concluded. "You're screwing your way to the top."

She rushed from the room — from her own shop — to the sound of all my plans backfiring.

∼

I THINK there must have been tears in her eyes as she brushed past Hector, who was headed toward us, into the shop. I started to go after her, but he stopped me — literally blocking my Constitutional right to the Pursuit of Happiness.

"This is way, way out of hand," I said, catching my breath and trying to push past him. "I've got to tell her the truth."

"Not so fast," he said soberly, shoving back. "So she thinks you're a gigolo. Tell her the truth and she's gonna know you're just a lying asshole."

He paused long enough to let the paralysis of my dilemma take hold. Then he said, "You're not a carhop anymore. You Rockin' Rollo, my man."

He said it like he already knew about Paragraph Nineteen Sub Two.

"Rockin' Rollo," I repeated, trying it on.

CHAPTER 21
EATING OUT

I was eager to see my room, but Hector said it wasn't ready. He mumbled something about a rock band checking out of the suite and those situations requiring special attention. Perhaps because he saw my frustration at not being able to make a clean breast of my intentions to Felicia, he suggested a late lunch at a posh place with umbrellas over on Cañon Drive.

It turned out that Hector had an expense account for entertaining VIPs. So as long as I was on Farnsworth's good side, which couldn't last very long, we decided to use it for its legitimate and rightful purpose — convincing a valuable guest that the management had no higher priority than the complete gratification of his every personal need.

I really started getting into the spirit of the thing as we sat at an outdoor table with a pricey bottle of white wine chilling in a Sterling-silver bucket nearby.

I was giddy from the alcohol, nearing the dizzying summit of my second climb to inebriation that day.

I stared down at my plate. The twin poached eggs should have reminded me of teacup-sized breasts but instead had me seeing a pair of Happy Faces. So I arranged the black olives as eyes and added thin sprigs of over-green asparagus to make smiles.

I didn't notice that the maitre d', a fastidious Frenchman named Louis, was standing just behind me observing my creativity with detached amusement.

Hector *did* see Louis and no doubt regretted the mistake of bringing me to a place where good manners are as expected as shirt and shoes. Showing his embarrassment, he asked, "*Pendejo* — just what do you think you're doing?"

Not taking his cue, I continued to play, inverting the asparagi to make my sunny twins scowl.

Thinking how I'd ruined my chances with Felicia, my playfulness took a sinister turn, and I jabbed my fork into one of the golden yolks. "Hah-*hah!*"

As I extracted the fork, a gob of runny yolk clung to its tines. Composing the triumphant speech I was about to deliver, I raised the fork in an exultant gesture, and the gob flew back, landing squarely on the lapel of Louis's immaculate uniform.

Oblivious to my mistake and concentrating fully on Hector, I continued to brandish the fork as I pronounced, too loudly, "Stinky fish eggs, dyed asparagus, smoked Norwegian pink zombie flesh, topped with poached cage-free organic eggs on little circles of gluten-free toast." I held up a sprig of cilantro, and I couldn't understand why such an innocent action should inspire a look of dread on Hector's face. "It's this licorice-tasting grass," I said. "They throw some of this on the plate and presto, the price goes up fifty bucks. What a rip-off!"

In this short interval, Louis had officiously left. It was his quick return to my side that had in fact caused the dark cloud to drift across Hector's brow.

I looked up to see Louis tightly clutching a small black leather portfolio to his chest and smiling too broadly.

There it was clinging to the satin border of his lapel — a sticky yellow gob. I watched carefully as it dripped down into his silk pocket-handkerchief.

I took a big gulp of wine, emptying my glass. No sooner had I replaced the leaded crystal on the table than Louis himself bent forward — pointedly brushing our waiter aside — and grabbed the sweaty bottle from the bucket to silently offer me a refill.

I, too, grasped the bottle firmly, and we had a little tug of war.

Giving up without a fight, he released his grasp as I said, "I prefer to pour my own, ah...?"

"Louis," he said helpfully, stretching his grin to its muscular limits.

"*Muchas gracias*, Looey," I said — pouring to overflow, and sopping the Egyptian linen tablecloth.

As I returned the bottle to the bucket, the purchase of my grip on its slippery wet surface went bankrupt. It plummeted to the bricks and shattered, drenching Looey's pant leg with the dregs of a $300 bottle of Bouchard Père et Fils Montrachet. (At least, I didn't injure my foot this time.)

Not only the little army of waiters but also my fellow diners glowered.

That pissed me off.

"What kind of social leeches have the time for breakfast all day long?" I demanded, glowering back. "It's not like the food is so great here."

To punctuate the conclusion of my remarks, I dropped the fork into my plate, signaling termination of my interest in the meal and this elitist establishment. The clang was so sharp, I expect the impact chipped the bone china, but I wasn't about to look.

"Rockin' Rollo," Hector said, hoping his laugh was contagious. "You on a sugar high? I told you not to eat the dessert first!" He added a guffaw for effect, but no one else was amused.

Okay, I thought, *time to rock, Rollo. They can't get away with this.*

Remembering some scene from an old movie, I snapped my

fingers smartly and pointed my finger at Looey's precious little portfolio.

He stepped forward briskly and handed it over, barely containing his glee that I would never eat lunch anywhere in his town again.

"I just happen to have your check right here, sir," he said, then added in a nasty, spitting whisper, "I do hope you have cash. It seems our credit card machine is down."

Judging from his throbbing neck veins and the manic look in his twitching eye, he was relishing the thought of grabbing me by the collar and tossing me bodily into the street.

"You gotta pen?" I yawned.

He obliged me — with a Mont Blanc, no less — even though he must have been wondering why I wasn't reaching for my wallet.

I signed the check with a flourish, printed my name carefully beneath, and, clapping the case shut, handed the portfolio decisively back to him.

With an accusing look, he made an elaborate point of retrieving his pen.

For a moment, he was frozen. Then, he opened the thing, took a peek, and closed it again.

There was no look of recognition on his face as he planned his next move. This guy was aces at poker, you could bet.

"If you'll excuse me just a moment?" he asked, indicating the check. His grin came back just before he turned and walked off.

It seemed he was gone a very long time.

"What's going on?" Hector asked. "I said I would pay."

"Nothing doing," I said. "This is Monica's treat."

"You *signed her name?*"

"Hell no," I said. "I signed mine."

"*Aye, yiyi.* Strike three. You gonna be away a long time, my friend."

It was a gamble, of course, but when Louis eventually strode over to the table, chuckling and all smiles, I knew that the CIA could not hope to match the stealth and efficiency of the Bel Air Movie Mafia.

"The manager sends your employer his warmest personal regards," he beamed. "May I add that it has been a distinct pleasure to serve you and your guest, Mister Hemphill?"

"*De nada,* Looey," I said with a pasted-on smile as I got up. "I trust you'll add a gratuity sufficient to compensate for any... ?" I waved my hand languidly to indicate the disaster area.

As long as all eyes were on us, we took our time leaving. As he followed us out, Louis pointed back to the courtyard obsequiously, "Next time, a corner table? Not so much sun?"

Seeing us emerge at the curb from his post a block away, Ernie pulled up in Monica's stretch and Everybody Who Was Anybody saw (or was later told) that Hector and I got in.

In the back seat on the curb side, for Louis and all to see, was a famous silhouette. So cool, so aloof — she stared straight ahead and didn't flinch.

As he watched us pull regally away, I swear Frog Looey was resisting a strong impulse to salute.

CHAPTER 22
IN AND OUT

One of the Honeypackers' stakeouts was rewarded richly when they saw the trench-coated figure emerge from Bungalow B late one evening. Keeping a safe distance away as they followed on foot, they saw the subject go right to a plus-sized Cadillac Escalade in the lot and drive off.

The next time he spied the Escalade, Woody was particularly resourceful in surreptitiously attaching a small wireless rig to the rear window and affixing the transmitter under the bumper with duct tape (called *gaffer's tape* in the trade).

So another day when a second, daintier trench-coated figure climbed into the truck for an outing, the ensuing conversation was captured with surprising faithfulness on digital audiotape.

Realizing their Winnebago was far too conspicuous for close-heeling on a tail job, Lucille and Woody followed a good half-block behind, but still within range of the transmitter.

The conversation is particularly revealing after the vehicle exits from the drive-thru window at an In-N-Out Burger and parks in the lot. From the sounds of rustling paper, munching, and slurping, it's safe to conclude that the subjects dined *in*.

"When we passed those notes in school, did you imagine we'd be together like this?" Monica asks.

"I hoped we'd get together," Merl says. "But like this? We were kids. Who knew the crazy things adults do?"

There's a pause. More rustling and slurping.

Finally, Monica asks, "Do you think Dennis would give you a divorce?"

Bingo. Dennis. Merl. Merle Cantwell. Yeah, all right, it took us a while to catch on, but now we were on the same page as the perps.

The Honeypackers would have gone straight to the media with this little tidbit, but fortunately for our purposes I had them firmly in tow by this time, and I was able to impound the evidence and advise them to let me control the timing of any news tips until I could build my case.

"California is a no-fault state," Merle says. "Doesn't make any difference what he wants."

"Well, then?"

Merle sighs. "Your basic pipefitter would not understand."

There follows a conversational void of some minutes.

Then Monica says, "We're not getting any younger, you know."

"Tell me about it," Merle says. "No more Double-Doubles. Cholesterol is for kids."

"Time is so precious now, Merle."

Taking the intended hint, Merle asks, "What are you trying to say? You got some kind of disease you didn't tell me about?"

"Age spots," Monica says. "Below the neckline, thank God. But it's only a matter of time."

"They got stuff for that," Merle says. Relieved that Monica's distress isn't caused by anything more serious than an everyday crisis of vanity, the mayoral candidate is clearly relishing the crime of dining out with special circumstances. "This is great," she says. "Where are you supposed to be just now?"

"Shopping," Monica says. "Clothes for him."

"This is great, I mean it," Merle says. "If the whole world thinks he's doing you, nobody cares what I do — at least, where you're concerned. And if they all think *you're* somewhere else, I can slip in and out of that bungalow as easily as a bellhop. I mean, we could do it in Macy's window, and no one —"

"If it helps you relax," Monica says, "it will have been worth it."

We hear the sound of Merle rooting around in her paper sack. "Like I said, this is great. Great idea. License to cheat. Big-time. Do you know how long it's been since I've done this? You gonna eat your fries?"

Sound of Monica siphoning the last of her Coke.

"No. Yeah, great."

Somebody belches.

CHAPTER 23
PARTNERS IN THE PRESIDENTIAL SUITE

While Monica and Merle enjoyed a bit of the old in-out, Ernie drove Hector, me, and the Pseudo Monica clothes shopping. Bored unless she was doing it for herself, she naturally stayed in the car.

I made out, lemme tellya. Armani this, Ferragamo that, topped off with a style cut and color rinse at José. I began to appreciate how much better shopping can make a girl feel at the worst of times. It was much more effective than drugs or booze — but a lot more expensive, of course.

I was signing Monica's name now, all over town. We had a contract.

When my entourage returned to the Palms, Ernie carried my purchases up to the tenth floor. Room 1098 was down at the end with a gleaming brass plaque on the door: "Presidential Suite." Hector was already inside, having carried the exhausted P.M. up the back elevator and arranged her prettily on a love seat in the living room.

Hector wanted to order up a champagne dinner, and Ernie was eager to join in, but I begged off with a headache. Ernie kidded me about just wanting to be alone with the P.M., but Hector, in his newfound role as my personal manager, shooed him out protectively and advised me to get some rest.

Of course, I was much too wired from the day's activities to rest. The suite was sumptuous — a mega upgrade from the boiler room I expected (and thought I deserved). But all I could think about was seeing how I looked in my new clothes.

I must have spent a couple of hours admiring myself in the full-length mirror, striking cover-guy poses as my synthetic patron looked on approvingly.

"A guy could get used to this," I said. "How do I look?"

If she objected, she'd say something. She didn't.

"Hey, it's plastic money and a rubber doll is paying the bills," I said. "What a country!"

Starting to feel satisfied with myself for the first time while sober in many a moon, I crossed to the coffee table and plucked a small aqua-colored jewelry box from its Tiffany bag. Inside that was a hinged plush box, and lifting the lid I marveled at the two-carat rock in its platinum setting. I'd had no idea what to get, but Hector assured me that the ring's eye-popping price tag was adequate assurance of its suitability.

"Oh, this?" I thought I saw a smirk of mild surprise cross those latex lips. "It's just a little something I picked up when you weren't, heh heh, looking."

She glowered at me, a look that was all the colder because she was still wearing her shades after sundown.

"All right," I admitted. "It's for Felicia. Kind of a friendship ring."

That much was true. Maybe the best I could hope for was friendship at this point, but I was willing to start there.

"No, I'm not the least bit ashamed of myself," I said, in answer to her probable question. "We played a pretty rotten trick on her, and if this can even begin to make up for it, you got away cheap."

She was thinking Felicia would guess how I managed to buy such an outrageously expensive gift, and that perception might further impugn her image of me, canceling the intended effect of the glittering peace offering.

"I don't care what you think," I said. "It's worth a try and you're backing me all the way. She's pretty mad at me, you know. I wanted her jealous, but this is ridiculous."

The P.M. was jealous, too. That explained her nasty attitude, which gave no sign of encouragement.

"Don't give me that," I said. "There's not a jealous bone in your body. There are no bones in your body."

In fact, she was formed over stainless-steel rods, far stronger than bones, strong enough to withstand anything I could throw at her.

But I wasn't about to oblige.

But even if I had, what's so wrong with any sex that doesn't make unwanted babies or spread disease? It doesn't take high technology to prevent either, and yet there's so much of both. But here I was locked up in a room with a sophisticated marvel of modern fabrication, designed for lonely humans who can't find even one willing warm body among the billions of others on the planet.

What kind of person buys these things? Who would debase themselves by demanding such a lifelike yet utterly lifeless physical form upon which to gratify their crazed sexual urges?

(Burn victims.)

CHAPTER 24
PERKS FOR PERPS

The next morning, I stood out in front of the Palms, admiring my new manicure (my first one ever, but sadly, not done by Felicia) and waiting for Ernie to collect me. I knew I was on assignment today, but I didn't know where he would be taking me, er, us. However, the P.M. was nowhere to be found in the suite when I woke up, and I figured they'd taken her to get "dolled up" for our day out. Maybe, as they'd done for me, they'd gotten her a new outfit. I caught myself wondering how she'd look in it.

I had the suit, the shoes, the gold watch. Everything Stan had except the low IQ and the shit-eating grin. You'd think it would have made a difference, but here's what happened when I ventured downstairs.

"Mister Big Shot," Laszlo said resentfully as he gave me a disapproving glance.

As he turned away and sauntered into the lobby somewhere, who should walk out but Felicia.

On seeing the new me, she remarked, "It's amazing what a fresh coat of paint and a little landscaping can do."

"I haven't done anything wrong," I said, meaning it as a conversation opener rather than a rebuff.

I hadn't expected to meet up with her here, especially not when I was presumably waiting to do a stint as celebrity lap dog. But I didn't know how to push her away — didn't *want* to push her away.

My paradox kept getting more paradoxical.

"If a lie gets repeated often enough..." she began, "but then you'd know all about that. Are you going to remember your friends?"

"Friends?" I asked. "Is that what we are?" It came out plaintive, but, from my viewpoint, I was being hopeful. We'd at least have to make it to friendship before I could offer a friendship ring. (Under the circumstances, rushing straight into a proposal was out of the question. I mean, in the off chance she accepted, how would I explain where I go to work or why I can't give up my mistress?)

Her answer wasn't an answer, but a hurtful accusation: "You only ever had one enemy, Rollo. He wears her clothes and eats her food. Watch out for him."

Before she could stomp off, we both caught sight of a new shiny red Porsche Turbo Carrera convertible as it roared into the drive and pulled up in front of us with a faint squeal of its precision four-wheel discs. Ernie jumped out and tossed me the keys. Instinctively, I reached over to the carhop's rack and plucked off a fresh ticket. (I imagined Laszlo was enjoying this from a vantage point inside.)

Tearing off the stub and handing it to Ernie, I said, "You know, I don't do this anymore."

He wouldn't take it, which pissed me off.

Is everybody playing with me today?

"Be a sport, Ernie," I said. "Laszlo's picking his nose someplace, so why not cut me a break and park it yourself?"

He just smiled politely. "It's still in the break-in period, so no hard acceleration and don't open it up on the freeway."

You still think I'm a joyriding asshole, you asshole?

But he wasn't teasing. He was beaming.

"Wait a minute," I said. "Are you trying to tell me... it's *mine*?"

"Not at all," he said. "It's in her name. You're just the, wuddya-callit, designated driver?"

He handed me a folded slip of paper. "Be there," he said. "Three o'clock."

With that, he walked off toward the bungalows, whistling.

Felicia didn't know what to think. Or rather, she knew what to think, but it made her sick to her stomach.

Laszlo showed up, probably having carefully timed his reappearance.

Assuming it was his job to park the car, he moved to grab the keys from me, but I held back.

As I climbed into the driver's seat, he haughtily assumed his position alongside Felicia at the curb.

"Some Mister Big Shot," I saw his lips say.

I MOTORED PLEASANTLY DOWN Sunset to Pacific Coast Highway. Realizing I had plenty of time before my appointment in Malibu, I stopped in at Duke's, treating myself to a few fortifying vodka tonics at the bar, followed by a Crab Louie salad, although just seeing its name on the menu brought back understandable feelings of resentment and hostility.

If I had any hope of redeeming myself in Felicia's eyes, it lay in becoming more myself, despite the elaborate outward sham I was now forced to project. If I could show her the real me — no, a new, improved *future* me nourished by gainful employment, buoyed by prosperity, and enhanced in self-worth — *if I could become a man she could love* — no lies, no matter how clever or widely believed, would stand up to the shining truth.

It was my ego that needed inflating, not with laughing gas or stale farts or cigar smoke, but with a clean, crisp breath of fresh air.

Right then, I resolved to acquit myself better, drink less, eat more fruits and vegetables, sleep more, and pick up some ritzy casual clothes so I didn't look like a Porsche salesman on his lunch break.

On the seat of the sports car, I'd found a Hugo Boss alligator leather card case with a spring-metal gold clasp that held five new hundred-dollar bills. Inside was an American Express Black card with my own (full legal) name embossed on it. I paid with the plastic, adding just ten percent for the barkeep as is no more than customary, proud that I'd behaved myself and therefore had no need to reimburse the establishment for broken crockery or hurt feelings.

The address on the slip was up the road in the Malibu Colony. I wondered why they didn't have me squire the P.M. in the open-air showplace of the new convertible, but I had no doubt she would be waiting for me, suitably attired, at the appointed rendezvous.

Things were getting complicated, but now at least I could concentrate on the job I had to do.

Ah, well. Showtime.

I had no idea.

A GUARD SHACK barred my entrance to the Colony, and in it sat a mild-mannered quasi-military man whose helpful badge said his name was Monroe.

He greeted me with a sincere smile as I pulled up.

"We've been expecting you, Mr. Hemphill," he said. "It's keyless entry. The code is your birthday, six-digit format."

Feeling myself about to slip down yet another rabbit hole, I just stared at him.

He laughed, "You can remember your birthday, can't you?"

"Yeah," I said. "I didn't know *you* could."

Oh, I was such a wit and he was just as good-natured. "Oh, it's all in the computer," he said. "Best to watch yourself," he added confidentially. "You don't want to get yourself erased. Her last boyfriend's in data heaven, if you know what I mean."

I nodded solemnly, not wishing for an early binary demise.

"Third gate on the left," he said with a comradely wink.

AT THE END of the third driveway on the left was an elegant beach house. Blocking my vehicle from the Japan-lacquered front door was a large wrought-iron gate. I tapped my key code into a control box, and the heavy gate swung open soundlessly.

I found a button for the doorbell at the center of a golden sunburst frieze embedded in the travertine marble facade. I pressed it and nothing happened. I waited, pressed again. Still nothing.

Beside the sunburst was a hinged lid, and beneath it, another keypad.

I tapped in my six-digit birthday, and an electric deadbolt in the front door retracted with a thud. The massive door must have been balanced perfectly because I pushed it open with the gentlest nudge.

The entryway was decorated with fresh-cut flowers in cut Steuben-glass vases and Impressionist paintings with authentic-looking brushstrokes beneath crackled varnish.

I stepped across the Italian terrazzo floor to a sunken living room. Its far wall was solid glass, floor to ceiling, with an expansive view of a stretch of white beach and waves breaking on volcanic rock.

The walls and furnishings of the large room were done in an art deco motif, comfortable and expensive, with no precious bric-a-brac. I was more than a bit surprised to recognize my favorite rock-band posters — the same ones I'd had at home — transported here and matted in shadow-box linen, encased in non-glare glass, and framed with African teak.

A freshly polished, full-sized concert grand piano didn't seem to take up much of the room.

Who was the old boyfriend, Billy Joel?

Was this my new world? Or a stage set where I'd play the fool for a time, only to get the hook?

A familiar head of red hair stuck up from an easy chair that was swiveled to face away from me. They'd sat her so she could look out over the ocean. How theatrical (or maybe more like daytime drama).

They've thought of everything. Even brought my friend so I wouldn't be lonely.

I walked up behind her chair and looked out, taking in her view. Waves of disgust were breaking on my beach. I took the ring box out of my coat pocket and laid it on an Eames end table.

My thoughts came out of my mouth: "I haven't had a chance to give it to her. I can't even get close enough, for long enough, to explain. Getting out of hand? Jeez, I've slipped into some kind of alternate universe."

Mindlessly, I let my fingers dangle in her hair. But when I ventured to caress her cheek — the flesh was warm!

"Yuck!" Monica said.

"It's you!" I exclaimed.

"What is all this caca-doo?" she asked, removing her shades and turning on me viciously. "Who do you think owns this place — the Car Jockey Pension Plan?"

"Wh-what's the idea?" was all I could say.

Jumping up to confront me, she snatched the ring box from the table and waved it in my face.

"Yeah," she sneered, her fist closing on the little package. "What's the idea?"

I grabbed for it, but she pulled her hand away. The ring box went flying, landing on the other side of the room. I wanted to go pick it up right then, but she stopped me with an excruciating knife point in the chest that turned out to be a manicured nail.

"I expected you to be surprised, pleasantly surprised," she said. "You know, like you'd just won the lottery? When could you ever drive a car like that if you weren't parking it for somebody else?

Instead all you can think about is spilling your guts to that bubble-headed little hairdresser of yours."

"Felicia thinks —" I started.

"I know goddamn well what she thinks," Monica said. "And she and everybody else in the known universe had better goddamn well keep thinking it."

"Am I supposed to live here with you?" I asked, troubled now about the implications of finding her here, waiting for me, in the flesh.

"Oh, it's Little Orphan Annie." She did her imitation of a whiny brat: "Are you my new Mommy? Do we live here now?" Then she was all business: "You'll be here or at the hotel. I'll tell you where and when. But not with me. Never with me."

I didn't know whether to feel rejected or relieved. "This is bizarre," I said.

"I don't sleep with carhops and I don't visit their tacky little apartments."

How did she know it was tacky? Weren't these my posters?

"Wait a min —" I protested.

"I'm not finished yet," she said.

"You have a helluva —"

"Now you listen to me —"

"What makes you think I'd even consider —"

"Shut up," she said, and that pissed me off.

Now more furious than intimidated, I started for the door. On my way, I picked up the ring box from where it had landed.

"I don't sleep with unemployed jerk-offs, either," she said, cutting me off at the door. "I date celebrities."

"What is that supposed to mean?" I asked, wondering whether, having discovered the ring, she now wanted to terminate my contract.

"Top forty, Rollo," she said. "Your interview is at four. If you leave now, you'll just make it."

How was it possible to feel hatred and joy at the same time?

"You just picked up the phone...?"

"They get to fire you after a week," she cooed, grazing my chin with the same lethal nail, "if you're absolutely awful. So it's up to you after all."

She took hold of my upper arms, as if to brace me for cold weather or schoolyard ridicule. "Don't screw this up," she said huskily. "Do what you're told, and you're going to get everything you ever wanted."

I weighed the little box in my hand.

"What about Felicia?"

Snatching and opening the box, she turned the stone to catch the light. Was she estimating its street value or imagining herself to be young again and so admired? "I appreciate your little gift," she said. Then with her head still bowed, she looked up at me with just a flick of her long lashes, and added, "Even if I did pay for it myself."

CHAPTER 25
JOHNNIE HALO

The appointment Monica had made for me was on the eleventh floor of the Capitol Records Building in Hollywood — *the heart of the music biz!* I didn't know whether it would be a job interview, an audition, or both.

Well, what had I prepared for, all these years?

It was the corporate office of a pop-rock FM station, and I was supposed to see one Johnny Halo, which was either a stage name or a really creepy alias.

The cute teen intern receptionist looked up from popping a zit and pointed down the hall to a door marked "STATION MANAGER." Behind it in a little waiting room heated by an overlarge computer monitor sat Verna, a pleasant-looking mom-type who, judging from her chest size and carnival makeup, had once been a showgirl. Now here she was plus a good forty years, which even if they were good probably weren't her best.

She bade me take a seat inside Johnny's office on an overstuffed leather guest couch. The chair behind his glass-topped moderne desk was empty, and the door to his private washroom was closed.

"He won't be a minute," Verna said, as she motioned for me to cross the borderline that divided conservative, tight-knit Berber from plush Karastan. On my way by her desk, she handed me the latest copy of *Billboard* with a knowing wink. Whatever I was supposed to know, I didn't.

Sunk too far down in Johnny's couch, I waited uneasily. I tried to run through all the rehearsed shock-jock routines I'd done in one parked car or another, but I came up empty, and, to make matters worse, I was beset with a cotton-dry mouth that had my upper lip sticking to my teeth Bugs-Bunny-style.

Johnny's office was all glass and black leather, about as inviting as a dentist's. On the wall, garish abstract art in splattered colors à la Jackson Pollock was intermixed with vintage shots of Motown groups. "I Heard It on the Grapevine," drip, drip. From this time capsule of his tastes in art, I figured the guy to be about sixty.

Ah, well — two decades younger than Farnsworth — this is progress, bosswise.

No use rehearsing, so I tried to read the magazine. I couldn't concentrate on that, either.

As I tossed it aside, I heard a faint whimpering from the washroom.

Moments later, the whimpering came again, louder this time, then modulated to a falsetto cry: "J-j-j-j... Johnny!" There was some panting, then: "Give. It. To. Me." *Squeak!*

"It's a bad time," I said to Verna, as I got up to leave.

She stopped me with a look. "He won't be long now."

There was the sound of a toilet flushing.

I resumed my place on the couch, and out of the washroom came the balding, middle-aged Johnny Halo, pulling up his Sansabelt slacks and carrying a folded, dog-eared copy of *Penthouse*.

I looked for some disheveled intern to emerge tugging at her skirt and straightening her bra, but no one else came out. He just switched off the washroom light and closed the door quietly.

"Ship sailed without you, sweetheart!" he called to Verna. "Again."

What hair he did have he wore down to his shoulders like an old hippie, with several days' growth of salt-and-pepper beard. He wore a Latin silk shirt unbuttoned about halfway, with a gold chain nestling in the profusion of chest hair that stuck out of it.

George Carlin with the soul of Larry Flynt.

He didn't take his seat behind the desk but slumped into the guest chair beside me.

"Who does she think she is?" he muttered. "She's not the only pair of tits in Hollywood with a degree in Microsoft Word."

Leaning forward to show him I was all compassion but not volunteering for a family therapy session, I said, "We could do this another time. Really."

He stared at me as if he'd just realized there was another warm body in the room.

"What's the matter?" he asked, throwing the girlie mag on the glass coffee table. "Never played with yourself?"

Did this require an answer?

"Of course not," he answered for me — patronizingly, I thought. "No need. You're boinking The Monica. How is the old gray mare?" Then, dropping his voice for Verna's benefit, he added: "Son, I was doing her when all she had up top was ginger snaps."

As his imagination fired on the image of twin spice cookies, he continued with renewed interest: "She let you touch 'em, or you just watch 'em go...?" He pantomimed boob jiggle, wagged his tongue, and cackled like the demented Mr. Hyde.

"It's not like that at all," I said, sounding like a high school sophomore explaining why he was out past curfew.

"I'd mind my back if I were you," he said. "Some powerful studs at that trough. A guy could get terminal hoof and mouth, if you know what I mean."

"Yeah," I said, realizing I had best agree with him. "Oh, but you have no idea how careful we are."

"Careful?" he asked. "That's right. Of course. Careful."

"It's almost like we're not even doing it," I said.

"God," he said. "Rubbers! I mean, what's the fucking point? At least you can feel the soft flesh of your own hand, know what I mean?"

He grabbed my knee and kept his hand there.

"Smart boy," he said with a knowing wink. "All kinds of crud out there. Masturbation isn't just for kids anymore."

"Not exactly my day, is it?" I said, dreading his next move.

"Not mine, either, pal," he said, thinking I'd changed the subject when all I was doing was filling dead air. "Damn Arbitrons. Shoulda stayed in goddamn auto leasing."

He grew serious, as though he meant business, and I wondered if that would also involve sex.

"Monica says you're some kind of fast-talking clown," he said, paying a high compliment.

"I know right now I don't seem —" I started to explain.

"I'm ready for a new asshole," he said, as though it were a job title. "And here you are, all sweet and pink and nice."

Gulp.

"Well, thanks, sir" was all I could think to say.

He jumped up, suddenly irate: "Don't gimme *nice!* Kids today, you gotta yell at 'em! They don't pay attention otherwise."

I was confused.

"You start on the graveyard shift," he said, calming down. "You don't put anybody to sleep who's not already, then we'll see."

Just like that? "I got the job?"

"I'm talkin' two ayem, you putz," he said, and laughed. "After a coupla days, you're gonna hate it, I guar-an-tee."

"Out-standing," I said.

He waved me out of the room, concluding another annoying task he'd manfully taken care of.

I was at the door when he said, "Oh, Rollo..."

"Yessir?"

"Take care, little man," he intoned with godlike concern. "That woman could chew the balls off a rhinoceros."

He was still laughing as I waved a hurried goodbye to Verna and raced down the hallway and into the elevator.

CHAPTER 26
ON WITH THE SHOW

The night of my first paid live radio gig, I paced the carpet of my hotel suite. I'd reverted to slacker attire — T-shirt and jeans — figuring I should wear comfortable clothes, but I was far from comfortable. I still wore the gold watch because, well, it was the only watch I had.

"I can't believe it. I can't believe it," I said on my sixty-third round-trip of the living room. "I'm on the air in..."

I consulted the watch and panicked.

"Ohmigod, *this watch has stopped!*"

"That watch got no second hand," Hector yawned from his place on the sofa beside the P.M. "So of course it *looks* like it's stopped if you check it every *two seconds*."

He was poring over a copy of *Daily Variety* while the P.M. was posed with a trashy paperback. Neither of them seemed particularly worried for me, as if they were killing time in an airport lounge.

"So what time is it?" I asked him.

"Same as when you asked before, plus *two seconds*. You know, smart money says you might try to catch a nap. You been up all day and now you're gonna work till dawn? You wanna keep that job, you just might want to get with the routine. You gotta be fresh, you know?"

"No, no, I'm too wired," I said. "But that's good. I'm ready. Wired and ready. I'll be fine. I'm gonna kill."

LEAVING the P.M. in the suite to catch up on her beauty sleep, Ernie drove me to the studio, and I was alert all the way.

I reported to the control room and met Jimmy my engineer, who showed me around. I'd expected to be spinning records and juggling tape cartridges — like I'd seen Robin Williams do in *Good Morning, Vietnam*. But because everything was under computer control, Jimmy handled the cuing of all the songs and commercial spots, which resided on the hard drive of a big server in a closet somewhere. The weather was prerecorded from the end of last night's 11 o'clock news — I guess on the theory that there would be no sudden drops in temperature or unexpected cataclysms until the morning shift came on. There was a traffic report every hour, but that was a direct feed from California Highway Patrol, so I had nothing to do with that, either. All I was supposed to do was make with some patter between songs and then introduce the next one, reading the song title off a computer screen.

I put on a pair of headphones and sat down in front of the broadcast mic. Jimmy gave me an on-air intro and I started the show.

Since it wasn't a call-in show, all I had was the sound of my own voice to keep things moving along. I knew the groups and some trivia about most of them, so I didn't have any trouble sounding like a veteran deejay. I mean, to myself, I sounded pretty good. And something I didn't expect — you hear yourself in the headphones, but richer and more resonant with amplification, which makes it all the easier to get off on hearing yourself talk.

I decided not to get outrageous with the patter, not at this hour and not on my first show.

Scattered around me on the table were the tools of the mimic's trade — perhaps left over from my predecessor — including various bells and whistles, even a miniature door with working knob for creating sound effects to accompany entrances and exits.

I felt like a soldier surrounded with loaded weaponry. I didn't want to have to use it, but I feared that circumstances would sooner or later force me to fire off an uncontrollable barrage.

The studio was equipped with an electronic clock, its glowing red numerals three inches high. A pulsing colon marked the division between hours and minutes, and as it ticked off the seconds, my eyes were drawn to its regular, hypnotic throb — especially when a tune was playing and I had nothing else to do but read the title and artist of the next selection on my screen.

At 3:46 A.M. — at which point I still had more than two hours of airtime to fill — I was fast asleep, or so Jimmy told me later. Behind the glass of the control room, he was doing a war dance. He was yelling his head off, which I'd have been able to hear if I hadn't removed my headphones as my eyes glazed over and I nodded off.

"Dead air, man!" a Tom-Thumb-sized voice screamed from the headphones (which if I heard, I ignored). "It's *dead air*. Jeez, wake up, will ya?"

He was still yelling as he rushed into the studio, but if I noticed, it didn't faze me. He started poking me (meanly, I thought groggily), but I easily slipped back into unconsciousness.

With the resourcefulness only a savvy technician could muster, he simply replaced the phones on my head and returned to the control room.

There followed a massive *explosion* between my ears. Jimmy had cued up a monster sound effect and cranked the level up way beyond ear-splitting.

As I recovered consciousness, my ears were ringing from the aural trauma. But I got the point. And I didn't dare fall back asleep or I knew the bombs would keep falling.

So, I improvised, "And that, dear ones, concludes our moment of silent mediation with the Reverend Sloan J. Sloane." Brief pause, then: "What's that, Rev? You just got here!"

I didn't even know I could do Billy Graham as I said in a syrupy drawl, "God bless ya. I gotta sunrise service in the Valley."

I slammed the little door to punctuate his exit.

"What dedication, folks," I said. "Ministering to our needs in the wee hours. That man never sleeps — but he rests in the arms of Jesus."

Hey, Jesus was a winning brand. Ask the neocons and Mel Gibson. No one was going to get fired for summoning the Lord's help on the air, particularly to an audience that was so freaked out *they* obviously couldn't sleep.

On the other side of the glass, Jimmy was on his feet, scowling at me.

"Now I think we'll do ten," and I stifled a yawn, "no — make that twenty — blasts from the past. These oldies need nooooooo introduction."

I gave him the "roll 'em" high sign, and he shot me a disgusted look as his fingers flew over his keyboard to bring up a creaky old blues number.

As the tunes rolled on, it took all my effort to keep from staring at the clock.

AFTER FIVE, at the end of my shift, Jimmy turned the control room over to another engineer and I ceded the studio to the morning drive-time guys. They were slurping black coffee from tall mugs with their show logo on them, and no one gave any indication that they'd heard my show or even knew who I was.

I stood with Jimmy at the coffee machine as we waited for a steaming cup to finish filling. He was remarkably subdued, I thought, after the fit of temper I'd inspired in him. When the coffee was ready, he reached in and handed me the first cup. I was so tired I had to lean against the side of the machine for support.

"Here," he said, helping me wrap my fingers around the cup and lift it to my lips. "You'd better get your shit together, man. I'm not about to save your ass anymore."

"I didn't do such a bad job," I mumbled. "Besides, the graveyard shift — who wants it?"

"Me," he said. "Me, that's who."

"Whaaa?"

"I was up for it," he said. "Then somebody pulled rank. So keep screwing up and I'll get my break after all."

It hadn't occurred to me that I'd competed with anyone for this thankless no-brainer show that no one listened to.

Who was my audience anyway? The cleaning crew vacuuming the train station? Unlucky hookers on street corners? Insomniacs who'd be better off listening to elevator music instead of hard rock?

With Jimmy's news came the anxious thought that someone may have actually been fired to make room for me.

"Jimmy," I started to say, but I was afraid to know the answer.

"Finish that," he said, my big brother now. "Don't want you running into a tree on the way home."

I didn't have the heart to tell him I wouldn't be driving myself home. His dusty Ford Escort with "Wash Me!" on the rear window had already left the lot when Ernie called for me in the stretch.

CHAPTER 27
SUCCESS FOLLOWS SUCCESS

Later that morning — it couldn't have been much past seven — Hector says I was snoring loud enough to call the hogs when he used his passkey to let himself into the Presidential Suite.

He startled me awake when he yanked back the drapes and a blinding shaft of unwelcome sunlight came pouring in. The brightness almost made me sick to my stomach, and I wondered if maybe vampires attack out of pure revenge for being roused during the day.

The floor of my bedroom was strewn with my upscale wardrobe, which Hector raced around collecting. He hadn't minded the mess last evening. I didn't know what had changed.

"Get housekeeping up to the Presidential Suite," he commanded loudly into his cell. "We got a truckload of dry cleaning up here."

Snapping his phone shut, he continued in his commanding tone, "Get your ass outta bed, *pendejo*."

Oh, shit. He's throwing me out!

"Ugh," was all I said, trying to extricate myself from the sheets, which I had wound around me.

I propped myself up on an elbow and he sat on the edge of the bed. Far from throwing me out, he appeared to be currying my favor. "Hey, Rock," he said, indicating the mess as though it spoke for itself. "You need a manager. Fortunately, you already got one. That'll be fifteen percent of your gross, and you can forget about paying off my Visa for that little party favor I bought."

"Lemme alone," I said, hoping I could fall back to sleep.

"No way, Jose," he said, grabbing my ankles to pull me from the bed. "You gotta go to work."

"Jus' got *off* work," I yawned, upset that my new manager was so apparently confused about my schedule. "Couldna been asleep fi' minutes."

"Some Johnny guy wants you to *vamos* down there," he said. "Pronto, bro."

Oh, shit. He's heard about the show.

I'd get fired, and I'd get evicted, and then Paragraph Nineteen Sub Two would kick in.

"I jus' gobback," I whined.

"C'mon," Hector said. "We gonna get you some coffee."

The word *coffee* triggered a synaptic firing in my brain, fusing a connection with the urgent pain in my bladder, and I had an urgent need to urinate urgently.

"Help me to the bathroom!" I pleaded as I fell out of bed, still hopelessly tangled in the sheets.

Hector half-carried me in the bundle of sheets to the bathroom, where he stood me up before the toilet and struggled to part the bedclothes so I'd have a path to pee.

As I started to let fly, I began to sag, and understandably my aim went astray.

"Ah!" he cried. "My new suede shoes!"

∼

Now officially empowered as my personal manager but operating without a contract to avoid any possible conflicts with Paragraph Nineteen Sub Two, Hector sat with me in Johnny's office.

Johnny looked different. Maybe it was the conservative worsted wool suit that definitely did not come from Walmart. He looked more powerful, and certainly more serious.

"It's the graveyard," he said gravely, "not a goddamn prayer meeting."

"I guess I —" I began, but he came so close I could smell his aftershave, and remembering the intimacy of our last meeting, I shut up.

"And *blues?*" he asked incredulously, closer still, giving off a waft of dissolving Altoid. "*B. B. King,* for chrissake? Him and Beethoven went to school together. Who told you to play that crapola?"

"I —"

"You know," Johnny went on calmly, "you don't have to work hard to put people asleep at four ayem." Just as quickly, he turned fierce, yelling at point-blank range, "You wanna *keep 'em awake!* Music to boink by, get it?"

Hector started, "Johnny, I'm sure we can —"

"I don't want to hear another word from you, cowboy," Johnny said to him.

"I guess that's it, then," I said quietly, remarking on my not particularly remarkable (except abnormally short) career in radio.

Johnny sat back down at his desk and put his head in his hands dejectedly, as if Verna had hidden his executive restroom key.

Hector and I were at the door when Johnny looked up and muttered, "I got nobody on drive time today. Fucking cokehead jocks."

"Excuse me?" I said.

"You're it, bonehead," he said.

"Sir?"

"Different ballgame. Top forty." He jabbed at me with an unlit cigar to emphasize each word: "No. More. Nice. *Abuse.* I want fucking verbal mayhem."

"You got it, boss!" Hector said, unnecessarily.

AT FOUR O'CLOCK THAT AFTERNOON, I was on the air. They'd put Jimmy in as my engineer — since he'd earned a rep as my nursemaid, I guess — and we both tapped into supplies of adrenalin that should have been exhausted sometime during the last shift and the umpteenth cup of black coffee.

He and Hector looked out at me in the studio through the control-room glass. They watched dumbstruck as I channeled rapid-fire patter from the ghost of Wolfman Jack, punctuating the routine with sound effects from my battery of playthings.

"Okay, thumbsuckers. Rollo's vocabulary word today is *pneumonoultramicroscopicsilicovolcaniosis.*"

Bell ring!

"A lung disease afflicting miners. So if you're under eighteen, watch out for this one! You get it from inhaling coal dust. Kiddies, remember, if the powder is *black,* don't snort it!"

Bicycle horn.

"Longest word in the Mother Tongue. Waydaminnit — tongue your mother? Don't try *that* at home."

Suggestive slide whistle.

"What am I saying?"

Slap! Bell. Horn. Whistle.

"Tune in tomorrow when we'll pick a mercifully short one — *antivivisectionists.*"

Cowbell.

"Hmmm. Fans of *I Love Lucy* who don't want Vivian Vance cut up into little pieces?"

Braying jackass (done by yours truly).

JOHNNY JOINED them in the booth. I could see their lips move, but I couldn't read the expressions, particularly the boss's solemn face. When Hector told me the first time, I didn't believe it, but here's how it went:

"Where does he get this shit?" Jimmy asked, probably figuring he'd have to distance himself from my performance just to keep his job.

"It's a pile of crap, all right," Johnny said with a deep sigh. He glanced down at the row of phone indicator lights. Every one was flashing, indicating the lines were jammed.

He arched a graying brow. "And they're eatin' his shit up like it was Rocky Road."

I WAS BACK in the suite by eight o'clock and all I could think about was stripping down to my shorts and falling into bed.

Hector was there to tuck me in, and he seemed anxious, which I thought was misplaced worry, under the circumstances.

"Tell me again why I even *need* a manager?" I asked, yawning. I dug into my shorts to scratch myself.

"Watch where you point that thing," he said. "You gotta know how to leverage your opportunities."

"Yeah, well, bite me," I said.

"What do you want, man?" Hector asked. "You get your first three hours of fame and you forget who your friends are?"

"All I ever wanted was for Felicia to think I'm somebody," I said and fell over onto the bed.

"I got news for you," he said. "You gotta convince yourself you're somebody."

As I stared up at the ceiling, the events of the last twenty hours whizzed by in fast-forward replay. "I was going to wipe out, and this guy Jimmy saves my ass. He was up for the same job. Why'd he do it?"

"Lots of people say they want to make it big," Hector said, sitting on the edge of the bed. "But what they really want is to talk about it. They don't want it to actually happen to them. Not really. Success is a big pain in the ass. What they really and truly want is to get close to somebody who's got it already. Like some of the glamour could rub off."

He could see I was starting to fall asleep, and I hated him for jostling me back awake. "You killed today, man," he said. "You keep it up, you get the regular drive-time slot, and your face gonna be on the side of every bus in town." He paused, deadly serious. "You're not ready for that, man. Nobody is."

As I started to nod off again, he got up and plucked a dry-cleaners bag from the closet and smoothed it out on the bed next to me. It was a full ensemble of black-tie dinner clothes.

"Go ahead, you get two hours sleep," he said, heading for the door.

"They got somebody else for the night shift," I groaned.

"I'll wake you at ten. We'll get you dressed, spit on your hair, and Ernie will pick you up."

"Where'm I going in the monkey suit?"

"You lucky little prick," he said. "You got a date with the real thing." He blew me a kiss and switched off the light as he shut the door.

This had me worried for a good two minutes before I fell into a deep, dreamless sleep.

CHAPTER 28
A CASE OF KEPPELHOFFER'S

Dressed to the nines, I waited at the curb for Ernie to collect me in the stretch. It was becoming a familiar routine — but with a troubling difference. This time there would be a living, breathing female body in the back seat. I was sure there wasn't anything in my contract about servicing the real Monica, but Hector pointed out that being seen in public with her would be good client relations (a poor choice of words, I thought).

As before when confronted with the thought of her as a sexual vampire, I was worried she wanted me, and worried she didn't. Was she just playing with my head? (It would be fitting justice, since I'd started it all by playing with hers.)

When the car pulled up ten minutes later, another difference was apparent right away — the figure of Monica in the smoked rear window was visibly animated. She was gesturing vehemently, no doubt giving Ernie some very explicit instructions. An obvious flaw in our ruse occurred to me then: *Who could ever believe Monica LaMonica would sit absolutely still for even a few minutes?*

When I climbed in next to her, I was struck by yet another difference between flesh-and-bone and silicone-and-steel: The sweet smell of Passion wafted over me. It was a warm evening, she was clad in her trademark snow-white fake fur, and her steamy, dewy skin gave off a rich, animal smell that made the air in the small compartment heavy as her perfume mingled with her own musk. Monica's funkiness was another stimulating and unnerving complication in what would prove to be a complicated night.

As the car sped off, she didn't acknowledge me right away, preferring to check her glossy, red lips in the makeup mirror. As she puckered and fastidiously dabbed the corner of her mouth with her pinkie, the fur parted to reveal a formal evening gown in sequins and silk with plunging neckline that amply showed what her pushup bra was carefully engineered to sculpt and support.

After a little pucker that I interpreted as a satisfied kiss to herself in the mirror, she turned her heart-shaped shades in my direction. I braced for a hit from the high-powered beam, but she just gave the space next to her a little pat. As she did, the diamond of her new ring flashed prettily, and I was at a loss to tell whether at that instant she was smiling at me or sneering.

Ah, Felicia, it was meant for you!

But this was here, this was now. The thrill of moving so physically close to the megastar made me take an involuntary breath. My nostrils flared, filling my head with her smell and making me momentarily dizzy.

"Keep your hands to yourself at all times," she cooed. "Unless I tell you otherwise."

Otherwise what? How should I respond? Express my disappointment? Shove my hands in my pockets?

"Uh, yeah, fine" was all I said.

"At the party," she said, assuming a businesslike tone, "you will be by my side at all times. You will not mingle. You will not — above all — give any other woman the slightest attention."

She paused as if waiting for me to initial this change in our contract.

"If you say so," I said.

"You are to look at me adoringly. At my lips. At my breasts. Especially here," she said, motioning from the nadir to the apex of her cleavage, "where they swell up out of my gown."

I had no trouble following. "I see," I said.

The emotional disconnect between her words and her subject matter was remarkable, as if she were a skilled surgeon describing my scheduled abdominal procedure in clinical detail when in reality she was planning to disembowel me viciously with a dull knife.

"Let's be very clear about this," she said. "You adore me. Whenever I'm not working, we're doing it. I excite you constantly. Your endurance is phenomenal. No sooner are you spent than you're engorged again with crazed, roaring lust. You can never, ever get enough of me."

I swallowed hard, crossing my hands on my lap to hide the onset of an erection. I assumed she expected me to speak, but I had no idea what to say.

"This is all by way of background," she continued, glancing down at my folded hands. "You must be totally convincing. My reputation — my whole *career* — is at stake."

She looked down again, and this time I worried I'd take a laser blast in the pants.

"You poor boy," she soothed. "All this pretending must make you rather horny. Do you miss your little Sicilian slut?"

"Now wait a min —"

"It's simple," she said, in a flash of ferocity. "Do exactly what I tell you to do, and we'll all get exactly what we want."

I nodded.

"Mess up," she continued, "and the only scoring you'll do will be with Miss Rubbermaid."

When we arrived at the Brentwood mansion of Joyce and André Dupar, the charity benefit they were hosting had been in progress for several hours. Monica clearly intended to follow the time-honored showbiz rule that stars should arrive late and leave early — well after financial contributions had been solicited at a late supper, but before anyone fell into the pool.

Like a swarm of killer bees that fed on alcohol, there must have been hundreds of guests converging on the lawn, patios, and inner sancta of this rolling estate. Uniformed keepers bustled among them, replenishing drinks and carrying trays of finger food, in case any of them had the slightest room left in their distended stomachs after an eight-course meal.

You'd think our hosts would be buried deep within the hive, but Monica must have been anxiously expected because when we pulled up they were all over the limo like fleas on a sweaty dog.

"Joyce, André," Monica said graciously as she got out, extended a hand, and hugged each in turn. "What a glorious do, and for such a good cause."

"Monica, you look stunning," André said, obviously meaning it and not minding that he'd copped a snootful of her perfume in the bargain.

"Do you know my beau, Rollo Hemphill?" she asked, mainly for Joyce's benefit, as Ernie helped me out.

"You'll be hearing him on the radio," Monica explained, taking my arm. "That is, your kids will. He's huge with Gen-Y — a very funny, a very *creative* man." She caressed a lock of my hair. "You have such *imagination*, don't you, darling?"

As she slipped her other arm through Joyce's and we walked up the path toward the big house, I heard her confide, "He can go for *hours*. My dear, I can hardly *walk*."

As we blended into the swarm and our hosts made to take brief leave of us, I heard him say to her, out of Monica's earshot: "I heard he was a car jockey."

"Well," his wife said, "he's got hold of a racehorse now."

As we turned away from Joyce and André, whom should we find but Audrey blocking our path. She was looking remarkably pretty in a new frock that must have seriously burdened her expense account.

"Hi-ya," she said to me, gesturing with her drink. "Miz LaMonica," she nodded to my glamorous date.

"Aren't you...?" Monica asked, as if she needed help remembering a name she had written in blood somewhere.

"Audrey Skolnick, slime of the earth," my ex said.

"Yes," Monica said, making a show of placing the name. "The... journalist."

"I came with a friend," Audrey said, mostly to me, gulping her drink.

"Lots of young women experiment," Monica said. "It's nothing to brag about."

Audrey is quick, but it took her a long moment to realize the naked cattiness of the gibe — unusually mean, even from this source.

"Can I print that?"

"Which is better," Monica asked her, "a short, sensational career or a long, luxurious one?"

Humbled, Audrey did a contemptuous take to me. Then I followed her eyes as they shot over to Felicia, who was an angelic vision, backlit in the golden light from a patio door, having just come out of the house.

She looked absolutely kick-ass gorgeous. They must have both burned through the last of their dough shopping for new gowns, and hers clung to her round places like silvery paint.

Brought here by Audrey to see her worst fears confirmed, and now presented with all the proof she cared to see, she was furious. At me.

Preempting any apologies or excuses I might offer, Monica approached her first.

"Why, Felicia, new outfit? Saved our pennies?"

"Yeah," she said in my direction, "weddings and *funerals* I treat myself to something new."

I was in anguish. I wanted to speak to her, and I looked over to Monica for permission, but the twin lasers flared and I was silenced.

"Give her the slightest encouragement," Monica whispered in my ear, "and you'll be living on a sidewalk."

To compound the misperception of my sins, she finished by nibbling on my ear. My head down, all I could do was stare at her cleavage.

Oh, well, at least I'm following instructions.

Noting our intimacy, Audrey sneered at me, "Planning a big contribution to Keppelhoffer's Syndrome?"

I must have looked confused, and I felt sick.

"If you'll excuse us," I said, "I think I feel a case coming on right now."

As I pulled Monica away from them, Audrey called after us, "Caught your show!"

"At least, we think it was you," Felicia added. "It was quiet for a long time."

And they giggled, sending stabs of humiliation through my body. Relieved I was no longer experiencing the pain of an unbidden erection, I felt a stomach ache and realized my last meal had been a half-eaten room-service sandwich at lunch.

I snagged a canapé from a passing waiter but I didn't get it into my mouth because I was distracted watching the girls over Monica's shoulder. Seeing this, Monica gave my arm a vicious squeeze, and I dropped my only chance at nourishment.

"Watch it, Rollo," she said, and was suddenly inspired: "I have an idea. Take me upstairs."

"They got a band up there?" I asked, knowing full well she had no interest in teaching me to salsa.

As she steered me up the interior stairs, she kept looking back furtively to make sure the girls were following.

"Not so fast," she said, slowing my progress. "We don't want to lose them."

Other guests noticed us, too, as we made our way through the crowd and up to the second floor, down the hallway, and into the spacious and elegant master bedroom.

Monica stopped at the door to a walk-in closet. I couldn't tell for sure, but I suspected Audrey and Felicia were just outside in the hallway, waiting for an opportune moment to peek in.

"Okay, I give up," I said. "What's in there?"

"Most of last season's shabbier designs," she said, without a hint of irony.

"I don't get it," I said, stupidly.

"Oh, you will," she said, as she opened the door to reveal wardrobe racks with more frocks than the Juniors department at Macy's.

She shoved me inside, then slammed the door shut on us.

"Well, you've heard of a quickie, haven't you?" she whispered in the darkness.

"I, I, I admit I'm, I'm aroused by you, all this," I fumfered. "But I didn't think, at least you said, I thought it was all pretend. I don't know if I can, or I, I, won't..."

"You don't think I'd let you actually *do* it?" she asked, making me feel smaller than ever.

I thought I heard giggles on the other side of the door, followed by some pushing and shoving as eavesdroppers jockeyed for position.

"Say 'I want you, Monica,'" Monica whispered.

"I want you," I said, being careful to keep my voice down.

"Louder!" she coached.

Reluctantly, I said, "I want you, Monica," loud enough for them all to hear.

"Make me believe it," she spat and fed me my line: "'I have to have you right here, right now.'"

"I can't say that," I said modestly.

"You've blown it with her," she said quietly. "You might as well have the last laugh."

True enough! Might as well go all the way!

"I have to have you," I said boldly. "Right here. Right now!"

I regretted my decision immediately, but once you start in, you don't want to stop.

"Oh, oh, baby!" Monica exulted.

She backed up against the closet wall and started to pound it rhythmically with her fists. With each thud, she emitted a little squeal of joy.

"Ah," she luxuriated as an imaginary me hit her imaginary sweet spot, "that's it. Ah ah ah ah ah ah ah..."

In my mind's eye, I saw Audrey and Felicia, listening in rapt disbelief — and disgust.

"Oh oh oh oh oh oh," I said.

Getting the hang of it now, together we yelled, "Oh ah oh ah oh ah oh ah oh a OH AH."

"Tell me I'm the *best*," Monica hissed.

"You're the best!" I exclaimed.

"Mean it," she said, cuing every piece of brass in the orchestra.

"Oh, baby!" I screamed, "you're the *bessst!*"

"Rollo," she gushed, as though she meant it, "you excite me so."

As if to lend reality to this statement, she emitted a throaty, "AAAAAAAAAAAAAAAH" followed by aspirated pants, "HEH-HEH," and a long, satisfied "UHHHHHHHHHHHHHHHHH!"

Deciding enough was enough, I interjected a manful "Uh," and we both fell silent.

At that point, we were really panting, perspiring in our nice clothes, just as out of breath as if we'd done it for real.

The room wasn't totally dark. A narrow band of light spilled in beneath the door from the lit bedroom. My eyes had grown accustomed to the dimness, and I could see Monica across the little space from me, her voluptuous bodice heaving.

Just then, she grabbed her chest, a look of discomfort crossed her face, and she seemed to have trouble catching her breath. Concerned my imaginary thrusting had actually taxed her endurance, I moved toward her, but she dismissed it with a wave of the hand and smiled, as if to say, "Good show."

"Say I was terrific," she whispered, gasping.

I hesitated, then went for it. "Babe, you were terrific."

"Now say you love me."

That is not in my contract!

I waited, too long, and she made such an ugly grimace, I had to summon all my reserves of acting talent to say with conviction, "I love you, Monica."

There was a scuffle outside. Monica glared at me, signaling my performance did not yet satisfy.

"I love you," I called out, making it real by picturing Felicia instead.

Someone on the other side of the door ran from the room.

Monica threw the door open and dragged me out, clutching my face to her, giving me my first taste of those perfumed tits.

Audrey was standing there.

"You know," she said, "I was sure I left my coat in here."

Monica planted a big, smeary kiss on me, then said huskily, "It's too hot for a coat, sweetie."

Audrey ran out.

We took our time making our exit, straightening our rumpled clothes — but not too much. As we emerged into the hallway, we had to push through a small throng of guests, and it dawned on me they'd been part of the assembled audience in the bedroom.

One of them, a short, middle-aged fellow, weaved in a swoon of drunken admiration as he stared unashamedly at Monica.

"What do you want, little man?" she demanded.

"An autograph?" he wondered, then realized he might do better.

He cackled: "A turn!"

CHAPTER 29
LIVING THE ROLE

The little improv Monica and I had acted at the Dupars had the effect she intended: It validated our cover story. The gossip about us now had a basis in observed fact. We were officially an item, and, since our relationship was no longer a matter of delicious speculation, it retreated from the tabloid headlines to the inside pages, alongside where-are-they-now stories about childhood actors of yesteryear turned aging, hopeless junkies — desperately seeking the next fix in a vain effort to replace the lost adoration of millions of fans.

As directed by Monica and coordinated between Hector and Ernie, I continued to date my synthetic woman, subject to the demands of my very real career as a drive-time radio personality. Monica was therefore free to see Merle, which I presume she did, subject to the soap's shooting schedule and the candidate's calendar of public appearances.

In short, everybody was busy living his or her respective lie and getting or not getting it off according to plan. My radio show proved to be hard work but had its perks and rewards, and even my ersatz social life fell into a routine that began to feel like reality — except for those times I'd catch myself staring at the P.M. and wondering what she was thinking.

Oh, by the way, my drive-time patter was winning me fans, ratings, and even an improbable rep as a sex idol. Comparisons with Howard Stern were unavoidable, but I was judged better-looking, less substantial, and more packageable. After I'd spent just two weeks in the time slot, Crazy Jay, the guy I was subbing for, took an extended leave of absence for health reasons.

Look at me. I'm the disease of the week.

Hector gifted me with a rosewood briefcase to mark my promotion to the ranks of sleazy respectability. I used it to carry a banana and a couple of cans of Red Bull to work, just in case I needed to push my raging blood-sugar level over the top.

Although Hector and I had retired my blowup doll when we replaced her with the custom-order dot-com rubber job, I was still dogged by my other inflatable friend — a swelling ego. After all, I could be deservedly proud. I'd achieved all my short-term goals: I'd made Felicia jealous. I'd even convinced her I was man enough to satisfy Monica's voracious sexual appetites. I had a paying job at a major radio station (with automatic deposits into my new checking account), an expense account underwritten by The Monica amounting to triple my aforementioned salary as on-air talent — *and* unlimited tax-free use of the Presidential Suite at Wuthering Palms, a beach house in Malibu, a chauffeured stretch limo, and a Porsche Carrera that still had its new-car smell.

I had everything I'd ever dreamed of and a great deal more — except the sweet and sincere love of the girl of my dreams.

And — small detail, irony of ironies, and despite the prodigious reputation of my public persona — I was the only person in this whole scenario who in reality was guaranteed to get absolutely *no sex at all!*

I could understand what had driven Johnny Halo into the closet, even though I didn't see what he saw in himself.

LIVING THE ROLE

TENNIS IS A LOT LIKE LIFE. It's a game you play mostly with yourself, and the other players are more than happy to take advantage of your mistakes.

Never an athlete, I whiffed Monica's passing shot as she knocked it expertly down the alley.

"Game, set, and match," she said, as if I cared about the score. She blew a kiss and met me at the net.

"My backhand's not working today," I said, recalling some sportscaster patter I'd heard on TV.

"My winning shot was to your forehand, Rollo," she said, toweling off as we strolled from the hotel court.

It seemed I was fated to always be working her into a sweat, but never for my benefit. Our biweekly tennis sessions were for show, to convince anyone who was still paying attention that she was still paying attention to me.

"We'll keep practicing," she said sadistically, "until people believe you let me beat you."

Oh, they'd have no trouble believing that.

AS WE STRODE across the patio area by the pool, all the better to be seen by lounging guests, Nigel passed by carrying a tray with orange juice.

As he gave me a knowing wink, she stopped him, grabbed a glass, and gulped it down greedily.

Almost immediately, she gagged, doubled over, and came up fighting for air, wheezing like an asthmatic.

"That was a Mimosa, you moron!" she gasped, lasing Nigel to cinders. He dropped his tray, juicing the lawn, and ran for help.

"Everyone, everyone here knows I can't have champagne," she whimpered and collapsed in my arms.

Moments later in Bungalow B, Monica was stretched out corpse-like on the bed. Dr. Ito, the hotel physician on call, was bending over her, gingerly applying his stethoscope to her famous chest.

Hector stood with me at her bedside, ready to take the news of her recovery to Farnsworth. Ito came over to him, shaking his head in bafflement.

"Not champagne, I think," he said. Then, tapping his forehead cryptically, he added, "*Taste* of champagne."

Ito saw we had no idea what he meant.

"No worries. I gave her antihistamine." He shrugged and was quick to leave.

Audrey and Felicia were standing outside the bungalow, waiting along with a gaggle of paparazzi for any news of the star's condition. Ito had given them nothing, and they were hungry.

I was still in my tennis togs. Audrey led the pack as she charged over and asked, "What'd you do to her?"

Mainly for Felicia's benefit, I replied, "Whatever you think I've done to her, now or ever, I haven't."

I went back to my suite and ordered room service. When Nigel showed up, I told him he'd done nothing wrong that I knew of and magnanimously directed him to add a big tip for himself to the bill. He was relieved and pleased, but then he wanted details about Monica I wouldn't (hell, I couldn't) provide, and he probably thought I was rude, maybe even arrogant, when I sent him away abruptly with not a scrap of new information.

THEY STARTED me doing public appearances to promote my show, and, adding to the pain of my celibacy, I became something of a sex symbol to teenage girls. One Saturday morning at a shopping mall in the Valley, a throng of screaming teenies rushed the stretch as Ernie opened the door for me to get out. A couple of helpful security guards were on them right away and pushed them back far enough to prevent physical contact.

"Oooooooo, Rollo! Hey, Rock! Gimme some loooove!" they cheered.

Still inside the car, I was remarkably unflustered, actually delighted to have anything like a fan club, and I decided to milk the moment. I took the P.M. in my arms — her companionship was required for use of the stretch — and I planted a big one on her rubber lips. It took some clever manipulation by me as puppeteer to make it look like she was kissing back, but those articulated joints work just like a real neck and shoulders, and it was a helluva performance, I must say.

As Hector escorted me to the record store where more fans were waiting eagerly, he confided, "They're talking about the length of your dick and how long you can go, man. What they don't get won't hurt 'em, eh?"

I said, "We all got what we deserved. Audrey's a reporter because she's a dirt-digger and a gossip. And I'm a gigolo-for-rent because I got no morals. And you, you're a manager because you're a blood-sucking leech."

That'll shut him up.

"I don't know you anymore, man." he said.

"Maybe you never did," I shot back. "Aren't you going to tell me I forgot my little hat?"

A line of fourteen-year-old girls stretched out of the store. Each of them was holding a glossy headshot of me and waiting for a personalized autograph.

"Gimme some space here, okay?" I said to a girl named Moon who was aggressively shoving my face in my face.

"Maybe now you're a star, you think you can do better than Felicia," Hector said, indicating my fans. "They're a little young, but you got no morals anyways."

Taking him aside, I said: "I'm sinking here. Felicia's all I ever wanted. But the more this weird charade succeeds, the less chance I have with her. Thanks, just thanks for everything you're doing, bud."

Another girl pleaded, "Sign it, 'Love to Terpsie?'"

"Spell it?" I asked. When she couldn't blurt it out, I scribbled something anyway. "Here, close enough."

I signed several others, without looking.

"You can have any bimbo in this town, man," Hector said. Did he mean it to sound encouraging? Or accusatory?

"No, I can't," I said. "That's Paragraph Sixteen Sub Three. I can't put the moves on anything that has real flesh. If I spend all my time being a phony, how do I get somebody to care about me for who I really am?"

As we left the mall and headed for the stretch, a city bus cruised by, and on its side, my smirking face.

"I been meaning to tell you," I said, turning on Hector and pointing to the bus ad. "Not Rockin' Rollo. That's so yesterday. Make it say, 'Rollo Rocks.' Bigger, and on top. Earn your stinking cut, man."

As the bus stopped to discharge its passengers, he said, "Don't look now. The rest of your life just got here."

CHAPTER 30
MONICA RECUPERATES

Pugsley, here. Among the reporters hanging around Bungalow B waiting for news of Monica's mysterious illness were the tireless Honeypackers. As they plotted their next move, those rats were planning to jump ship. That is, they regretted their cooperation with the Bureau, and in particular they didn't like sharing their take with yours truly. (It didn't occur to them I was the one keeping them out of jail.) I don't know what passed between them specifically, but I got a fair idea.

"She's got a bad ticker, Lucille," Woody opines.

"That young stud's been riding her hard and putting her away wet, you mark my words. She should get out of the game."

Never one to point out Lucille's mixed metaphors, Woody plays along. "Good advice for us, too, you ask me," he says.

"You were never in no game I wanted any part of, Woody Honeypacker," she snaps. "Time was, being a fan was no crime. Now they call it stalking and we got our sorry, sagging butts in a sling. They can't prove nothing when all you got on you is a pair of field glasses. A person's got a right to an interest in birds and whatnot. But they get you with recordings, audio and-or video, and the jig is up. It's no game, nossir, not anymore. You're too good at what you did, you got it all on tape, and now that Pugsley fella has us working for the man for free."

"What's your point?" Woody asks, innocently.

"She gets out of the business, we can get out of the business, is my thought."

I suspect Monica was harboring a similar notion.

But curiosity got the best of the Honeypackers, whose stakeout outlasted the media's. After the reporters had all gone home for lack of interest, Lucille and Woody tailed Merle's Escalade to a tacky little no-tell motel in the back streets of Burbank.

The motel owner wouldn't have been the least bit concerned about the matrimonial status of the couple that checked in for an afternoon nap, but he might have wondered why they wore trench coats in the 100-plus-degree heat.

The audio recording in this case is passable, but some context is necessary to understand the action — or lack of it. Apparently, Monica and Merle spent several hours stretched out (presumably naked) on the bed, where nothing except conversation transpired.

"How long do we do this?" Merle asks, expecting it's a kind of foreplay.

"Shhhhhhhh!"

"I don't get —"

"Lie perfectly still," Monica says. "Think about my lush, pink, naked body — so close beside you, pulsing with life, wet with the juices of love."

"Oh, please."

"Don't I excite you?"

"When do we get to *do* something?" Merle wants to know.

"You are the knight and I am your queen," Monica explains. "You can never possess me. It's called courtly love. Isn't the tension delicious?"

Merle thinks about it but can't find any merit in her argument. "You know," she says, "if I want frustration, I get all I can stand at home."

"You want to have me and be mayor, too?" Monica asks, sounding annoyed. "If we get found out, I'll still be a star, maybe a bigger one. But what kind of future can we have? I'd chuck it all for you, Merle. You and a triple-wide mobile home. Would you do the same for me?"

Merle sighs, and we can imagine she sits up, ending the game. "Do you know how few women have any real power? I don't mean some second-guessed CEO. And I'm talking about being able to reach out and crush your enemy like a bug."

This is all the answer Monica is going to get. "By the way," Merle adds soberly, "sex games don't go with a dicey heart, my dear."

"It's not my heart," Monica says. "It's just a thing I have."

"What kind of thing? All champagne gives most people is hiccups, maybe gas — worst case, a DUI or knocked up."

"You know what you need, Merle?" Monica asks. "A little imagination. Some creativity. Mix it up, once in a while. I'm role-playing all the time, but you're stuck being you. And you don't like it."

"Politics is the art of the possible, my dear," Merle says, "and I got my hands full just coping with reality."

"Don't disappoint me, Merle," Monica says, trying to steer the subject back to core concerns. "I'm warning you."

"Warning me? What are you going to do, expose your little carhop as a pervert who gets off on life-sized dolls? What does that make you? This license to steal was your idea, not mine, sweetheart. Where's he hanging out right this minute?"

"*Tout le monde* knows I'm recuperating in Malibu," Monica says, possibly wishing she were there instead.

CHAPTER 31
SHOOTING CELEBRITIES

Ernie had driven the P.M. and me to the beach house, where Monica was presumed by the world at large to be recuperating from her attack. The cause went unexplained, and the speculation about it put us right back on page one.

Pseudo Monica and I lay stretched out side by side on beach chairs, clad in matching Hawaiian outfits provided by Hector, who obviously needed a way to both tease me and give expression to his sick sense of humor.

Ernie was in on it. He wore a white houseboy's jacket as he served me a tall, frosty cocktail from a tray.

"I got things to do, you know," I said, accepting the drink.

"No, you don't," he said. "This is it. It's what you do now."

"You just going to leave me — us — here?" I asked.

He glanced at the doll, who could bask all day and never worry she'd burn. "You're on duty," he reminded me. "So amuse her. It's supposed to be my day off, but I here I am mixing you drinks! I'm gonna have a beer and watch the game. I got money on the 49ers."

With a mocking bow, he retreated inside.

Left alone with the P.M., I rolled toward her and said, "Lemmy tellya about this book I'm reading, 'Female Psychology for Dummies.'"

I sipped my drink and surveyed the beach. Two children — a boy and a girl, both about twelve — were walking along the surf in our direction. She carried a plastic pail.

"Wow, I'm getting everything but laid," I complained to the P.M., taking a sip. "Yep, paying my dues, can't get into the club." Sip. "Million hot babes in the world, and they all think I got no time for them." Sip. "Practice safe sex?" Sip. "I don't have to practice. I do it for a living."

When the children came opposite us, the boy reached into the pail, pulled out a camera with a telephoto lens, and nailed us with a rapid-fire sequence of snaps.

I stood up, waved my fist at them, and they ran off, laughing.

"Using children. Guerilla tactics. Scum," I said. But my companion had heard it all before.

A FEW DAYS LATER, Monica sat at a little writing desk in her suite. She looked well and rested. The latest issues of the tabloids were strewn about her, and she seemed visibly pleased that she was headline news again. She was particularly taken with the color spread in *People* showing the candid photos from Malibu.

"Ken and Barbie at the beach," she said, admiring the shots. "Love the matching outfits."

She lowered the magazine to look at me. In contrast to her placid demeanor, I must have looked disheveled and weary. I hadn't bothered to shave in a while.

"I want out," I said.

"Did you read your contract?" she asked pleasantly. "Paragraph —"

"I've got an image, too," I said. "No more lying, no more sneaking around, no more great sex I'm not getting."

"If you want to be a great lover, you'll have to learn patience, Rollo."

"Rock. It's Rock now," I insisted. "Felicia hates me, by the way."

Monica seemed amused, crossed over to me, and grasped my chin as if she were about to plant a kiss. "How do you know, Rock? How do you know she isn't secretly thrilled you're enough for a demanding woman like me?"

She sat back down, and went on, "Felicia doesn't hate you. You hate yourself. That's a different problem."

"I'll tell Audrey the truth," I said. "About Merle. She never gets her facts straight, but they pay attention to her now."

"So," she said calmly, "you know."

She took a moment, then said, "My fans will never believe you. Contract or no, you're just another boy-toy with a bogus lawsuit. You'd say anything, and you've got no proof. My attorneys will say your contract is a forgery. Let's see — what else have you got?"

"I'll take my chances," I mumbled. "I don't need this."

She grabbed a wad of papers from the desk and waved them in my face. "Know what I have here? Bills. Bills for restaurants, clothing — for both of you — hair styling, manicures, my two-carat teardrop diamond ring, a hotel suite deep-discounted to a thousand a day, a luxury sports car — leased, by the way — not to mention your unpaid rent at my beach house and services of a chauffeured limo. And then there's Hector. Your personal manager says I owe *him!*" She consulted a spreadsheet. "You've gone through fifty-four thousand six hundred and seventy-three dollars and fifty-nine cents in less than a month."

Not particularly startled by the sum, she looked up at me. "How much do you earn making animal noises on the air?"

"Not enough, not yet," I said. "But those aren't my —"

"Not your obligations?" She sat decisively. "Your contract also says we can reimburse your expenses out of any income you derive from the exploitation of our relationship. I'm sure Johnny won't mind sending your paychecks to me instead. That's a start." She smiled. "And I'm sure I can think of a way for you to work off the rest."

"Slavery," I said. "I'm a wage slave."

Just when I thought our conversation, if not our relationship, was over, she said brightly, "Let's try you on television."

ON A SOUND STAGE somewhere in Studio City, Monica and I were locked in an embrace. She was perspiring.

From out of nowhere, the disembodied voice of the director said, "Cut. Ah, Rock. You're off your mark again. Makeup on Miz LaMonica please!"

An assistant appeared instantly to dab Monica's brow, touch up her lipstick, and spray back an unruly lock of her hair. I guess I looked okay, but the camera was located behind me, focused on her.

She was the brilliant media executive. I was a callow young man with a fresh MBA and stars in his eyes.

"How do I look?" she fussed at the assistant. "Did he muss me? Check my back. My lips, my lips. This shot is so close. Accentuate but not too harsh. Are you sure that liner isn't too dark?"

I stood there and silently rehearsed my line.

"Ready," the director's voice said. "Again from the kiss. And *action*."

Holding a newly sharpened pencil, I made what I hoped would look like intelligent notes on a pad. Monica stepped into the shot, grabbed the pad, flung it aside, and grabbed me in a passionate kiss.

"You have a lot to learn, Dick," she said, rubbing my chest as she took her time delivering the line. "But I can teach you."

That's my cue!

"I'll never be the brilliant media giant you are, Miz Rauch," I said.

"Call me Louise," she said.

The director interrupted, "Cut. Again. Rock, mean it this time, okay?"

Dab-dab, pucker, blot.

When we were rolling I said, "I'll never be the brilliant —"

"Lose the line," the director said. "Let's take it from the kiss."

So began and ended my soap-operatic career.

Hector found me on the tennis court. I was facing an automatic ball machine, which was serving me one forehand after another.

I thought I was getting better. He switched off the machine.

"About had enough?" he asked, and I knew he wasn't talking tennis.

As he came closer, he said, "I could have told you what was in your contract, if you'd bothered to ask me."

"I'm a star and I live like a king," I said, "but I can't make any money. When she dumps me, I'll be right back where I started."

"You got experience now," he said. "Let your manager find you another gig."

"One word from her and who would hire me? Where am I going to go? Antarctica?"

"What are you going to do?" Hector asked, as if I had any options.

"I could push her in front of a bus," I said, delighting in the image of my grinning face on the ad rolling over her lifeless body.

He could see I wasn't seriously homicidal, and instead of ragging on me, he smiled. "Listen," he said, resting a hand on my shoulder. "I got a job. I don't need to be the manager of somebody who can't look at himself in the mirror. It's about self-respect, man. Starts with honesty."

Is he telling me to breach my contract? Is he saying fifteen percent of the rest of my life is worthless?

As he walked away, he added, "Life don't give you too many practice balls."

The next week was Felicia's birthday. I didn't have the guts to go over to her place myself, and for sure if I did Monica would find out, so I asked Audrey to deliver my gift. I'd bought a picture book full of dogs, knowing the puppy eyes would melt her heart and hoping some of the love would rub off on her image of me.

I was surprised that Audrey seemed happy to do it, and she gave me a report. Whether it was edited, I don't know.

She took her friend a store-bought cake, and when Felicia blew the candles out, Audrey said she started to cry.

"Does this have anything to do with Rollo?" Audrey asked. "I should have made a party, and we could have dragged his lying ass over here."

She gave her my present, which she unwrapped daintily and perhaps cautiously, and, just seeing the watery look in the eyes of the Westie on the cover, she started bawling again.

"Don't tell me you have feelings for him," Audrey said.

Felicia reluctantly nodded.

"Don't tell me you're *in love* with the guy!"

Felicia nodded.

"Well," Audrey said, "there goes my nose for news."

"I guess I'm a sucker for losers," Felicia said, blotting her running mascara with a tissue. "I put him off because I wanted him to make it somehow. I mean, he had no *plans*. Then he goes and makes it by…" and here came the tears again, "making it with *her!* I mean, sometimes I think — I drove him to it."

"Lemme tell you about Rollo's scams," Audrey said, hugging her. "And this has got to be one. In the end, they never work. Or, they don't work out the way he thinks."

"A scam?" Felicia asked. "What kind of scam?"

"Don't hate me for not telling you this," Audrey said. "But back when he and I had a thing? I maxed a few cards, then I lost my job. I was in deep, deep shit. He hacked some computer or other and all the bills went to a dead person."

"No way."

"He did some time, but mostly he got probation," Audrey told her. "He could've ratted me out. At least, he could've told them he didn't have anything to gain, and maybe they'd have gone easier on him. But he didn't have the heart. No ambition? He thinks he's a goddamn genius — that guy outsmarts himself. I mean, he's too dumb to know what works for him. This Monica thing is some kind of scam, I'm telling you. I just haven't figured his angle yet."

None of this made her love me, but maybe she hated me a little less.

When Audrey told me how it went, I figured I had to take a chance. The day after her birthday, I waited until her customers were gone and I walked into Felicia in her shop.

She didn't panic when she saw me, and she didn't run the other way. It was a start.

"So, you're a big TV star now?" she asked, as if we chatted every day.

"I had one line," I said. "And it was cut."

I came closer to her and said, "You have no idea what I've been through."

She turned to me and said, tenderly, "Rollo, sweetheart. I know what you did."

So what have I been beating myself up for?

"You do?" I asked incredulously.

"You took the blame," she said, "like you did for me when I could have lost my job because of Monica. And it wasn't your fault — not then, not now."

"Oh, Felicia, you understand!" I blurted out. "I got the idea from you, but the result was so unsatisfying. Then Hector got this idea, and Monica loves it, but she's never satisfied —"

"What are you talking about?" she asked, and I realized she thought she knew, but she didn't.

So rather than try to explain, I thought she should see for herself. I asked her to come up to the Presidential Suite, and although she was wary at first, she finally agreed to go when I swore I just wanted her to meet someone.

"I want to show you everything," I said, hating my choice of words, as we neared the door with the impressive brass plaque. "You'll see."

As I inserted the plastic card and turned the knob, I said, "The kinky part is, I never had sex with anybody — or any*thing*."

No sooner had I opened the door to the suite than we heard a man's voice — muffled pants and groans — as he made his way arduously to orgasm.

"You boys partying up here?" Felicia asked, turning to leave.

As I charged in, I growled, "If that Hector —"

I flung the bedroom door open, and there, naked in the bed was Hugo Farnsworth, the rubber Monica cradled in his withered arms.

"Mister Farnsworth!" Felicia shrieked, peeking out from behind me.

"She's everything I ever wanted in a woman," he said frankly, and I realized I might be the only colleague who could appreciate his honesty, even if I didn't envy his choice.

One of the P.M.'s lifelike feet stuck out from beneath the bedsheet. Felicia advanced a step cautiously, and unable to restrain her curiosity, she reached out and touched the silicon skin, then recoiled immediately at the odd sensation.

After that, explaining the rest was fairly easy.

CHAPTER 32
IT ALL UNRAVELS

After the events of the previous evening, I'd have thought Farnsworth would have me thrown out of the hotel — maybe Felicia, too. Maybe he'd have us sign some kind of nondisclosure agreement. Or, he'd take a long vacation and then vanish into retirement.

Instead, Hector said he reported for work bright and early, whistling and uncharacteristically cheerful.

What's more, I didn't lose my radio gig when Monica tried to launch my soap career. In fact, Johnny was hoping any concurrent success would rub off and lather up my fan base. And, it almost did.

Even though the director cut my line, I got my closeup. And not just from the back. The slackers among my followers who had time to watch during the day noticed me, the word spread, and I started getting bytes and bytes of electronic fan mail through the show's website. (My youthful, environmentally friendly fans lead blissfully paperless lives, except with respect to junk mail and toilet visits.)

So it wasn't my inept performance — or even my lack of performance — that caused my video image to be erased.

No, it was Monica herself. She threw a world-class, ordureflinging tantrum when she found out about the email. Her fans are of a generation that still relies on the postal kind, which takes more effort and time to produce and deliver, and evidently on the day after the episode aired, my adulatory missives outnumbered hers.

That was that, and I was out.

I did make one more appearance, however. I reported as instructed to the set the next week and was required simply to stretch out on a hospital bed. The director said the less acting I did, the better.

"We need you to do what you do best, Rollo," he quipped. "Die on-screen."

PRIVATE HOSPITAL ROOM, INTERIOR, DAY:

Dejected and defeated, Dr. Marcus Wellborn (a distinguished, mature gentleman, soon to be Monica's new love interest), rests a pair of paddles on my chest.

INSERT shot of the flatline trace on the heart monitor, as it emits a steady BLEEEEEEEEEEEEEEP.

Shapely, short-skirted Nurse Derkitt, who has been trying every way she can think of to get Wellborn to take her in the linen closet, pulls the sheet over my face, ceremoniously ending my last closeup.

EXTREME CLOSEUP of Monica sobbing. Tears are running down her cheeks, but her mascara miraculously retains its edge.

PULL BACK to a WIDER SHOT, featuring her tasteful Evan Picone suit, done in a discreet, muted tweed with black velvet piping on the lapels.

IN A TWO-SHOT with my shrouded remains out of focus in the background, she crosses to join Wellborn at the bedside.

"I know you did everything humanly possible, doctor," she says worshipfully, touching his graying temple.

Taking her in his arms compassionately, he says, "With the young ones, it's hard. It's always so hard."

"We mustn't think about that now," she says, fearing his own turgor might never be able to make up for the magnitude of her loss.

Lying there underneath that sheet, I had cause to reflect.

What if I died, I mean, really died, today, right now?

I would want Felicia there to comfort me. I would want to feel her grip remain firm and steadfast as the nerves at my extremities ceased to transmit and I lost sensation and my own fingers slowly but inexorably lost their hold on her.

The last thing I wanted to feel was a teardrop of hers on my cheek. (I mean this in the sense that I *did* want to feel it, but not until I had no choice but to feel anything else — *not* in the sense that it was the least of my priorities, as a person who isn't thinking in detail about his last day on Earth might mean it. Wow, words seem so inadequate, when you have no words left!)

But after the last brain cell winked out, after the last, struggling heartbeat — what then?

I didn't worry about my soul in the hereafter — that adventure would unfold, or it wouldn't, depending on how many planes of existence may or may not exist and how convoluted are the mathematical enfoldments of the texture of our maddeningly complex universe. I knew nothing of higher realms, levels of consciousness, or dimensions beyond the unremarkable four of my everyday life. I couldn't guess what would happen to "me," and I didn't see how second-guessing The Great Mathematician, if there is one, would get me any better odds.

The mechanisms of life are way too engineered to have arisen by accident, and life is too cruel and chaotic to be anything but accidental. Oy, it made my head swim, and I had the silly thought of my severed noggin bobbing about in a sea of consciousness as aimlessly as a discarded cork.

Better to drink the wine, before it's time.

No, what I worried about as I contemplated my own demise was simply the net result of my earthly actions.

What I wanted — all I wanted — was to have made a difference in Felicia's life. I really didn't care what the others thought about me, but if pressed I'd admit that their good wishes aren't valueless, either. Maybe someone clever could find the comedy in all this, someday.

But fame, I realized, almost too late, is way overrated.

No question, I *had* made a difference in Felicia's life, but the result was not what I'd intended. Thinking back on cautionary advice I'd read somewhere about dealing with God, I knew now that I hadn't been careful about what I'd asked for — and I'd gotten it.

Flinging aside my shroud after the successful take — which I now hoped would mark the end of *all* my fictional lives — I rose up like Lazarus, fully appreciating the underserved blessing of being granted a few more breaths.

Felicia had touched the rubber foot of my dead desire. In that moment, she knew me for the bankrupt soul I was, not the imaginary monster I had created. She had recoiled from the sensation of synthetic flesh — *but not from me!* I wasn't sure she loved me — or that she *could* love me — or that I could ever *hope* to deserve anything like love from her. But she had begun to understand me. And, weird as that was, it was a start.

The Great Mathematician is giving me a second chance!

When I returned to the hotel from the TV studio, my drive-time shift was due to start in less than an hour. I couldn't get Johnny on the phone — Verna said he was in a "meeting" — so I had Hector call in sick for me and immediately regretted having to tell even the smallest lie. But I realized, and it felt like a germ of wisdom, that I would continue to disappoint myself in many ways, and I should just get over it.

I switched on the radio — why not?

I changed into the only clothes in the suite that didn't feel phony, the T-shirt and jeans. Nigel brought me a bellhop's rack, and I started loading it up with wardrobe items from the closet.

I don't know why I was surprised to see Pseudo Monica still there. I had a mental image of her eloping with Farnsworth. But there she was, propped in her usual place on the love seat, wearing a smart set of khaki sports clothes set off with a bright, lime-green scarf. I don't know who dressed her — maybe Monica had hired an unseen servant or Hector was just showing off his fashion sense — but whoever had taken such care setting her out had, for the first time since we'd been together, left her glasses off.

Her glassy stare accused me, suggesting I was about to betray her.

"This isn't about Farnsworth," I said, after Nigel had gone. "I have no hold on you. You're not exactly a virgin anymore, and I can no longer be responsible for how you choose to make your way in the world."

As I continued to remove clothes from the closet, I sensed disapproval mixed with anxiety, much as the family dog will watch its guardian pack a suitcase and wonder whether the future holds a long ride in the car or a short trip to the kennel.

I noted her look of alarm when one of her favorite dresses joined my silk shirts on the rack.

"It all goes back," I said emphatically. "Goodbye, Halston. So long, Gucci. Nice knowing you, Givenchy."

I paused in my labors. Our relationship was a fiction, true, but the conversation I was having with her was real. I imagined she had feelings, and my intuitions were probably no more correct than those I'd had about Felicia's state of mind in any one of our past encounters. I'd probably been wrong most of the time about Audrey, too. If people don't, or won't, or can't express their feelings to us, we can and should react to whatever we imagine them to be. If we guess wrong, the conversation will be over sooner rather than later. If we get lucky and guess right, things start to flow and we have a rapport.

But, either way, it's a guess — whether you prefer to call it intuition or nonverbal communication or sympathy. If you're right more often than wrong, you're "sensitive." The other way, you're a self-centered jerk-off — take it from firsthand experience.

The P.M. inspired a Zen-like epiphany in that moment: The guessing is like swinging at pitches. The more you try, the more likely you'll connect, sooner or later, even if you strike out a lot.

I sat down next to her, increasingly aware that I needed more practice. "You know what I used to like most about you?" She modestly didn't answer, but she was ready to be reassured. "A little spin around the block and you were happy. We went places. We had a few laughs." I chucked her under the chin, and I thought I saw the hint of a smile.

She was beginning to see the humor in all of this, I was sure of it. "You were the slickest scam I ever pulled," I confessed. "And the stupidest."

She didn't share the laugh, but she didn't disagree.

"Hear that?" I asked, hearing the lead-in to my show on the radio. I went over and turned the volume way up.

"Thiz Jimmy B on your Super Station," a familiar voice wailed. "And a very special howzithangin' tonight to my main man Rollo, who got himself a bad case of the flu. Right back at you, my brother. You seriously sick, and I mean that in the best way."

Not wanting to listen to my competition lest I make myself genuinely ill, I switched off the set, and it occurred to me now would be a good time to try Johnny again.

This time, Verna put me through right away, after sincerely wishing me a speedy recovery. I thought she was sweet to think I'd told the truth.

When he came on the line, I said quickly, "Listen, Johnny. About the gig? My show? I'd tell you to go fuck yourself but you're doing a good job of that already so let's just say it's been fun."

And I hung up before he could answer or I could take it back.

There was a long pause, and I sensed the P.M. was trying not to laugh.

"Yep," I said, taking a good look around the elegant rooms for the last time. "Alone. Hotel room. Rubber doll. Unemployed."

CHAPTER 33
IT'S ALL ABOUT HER

Before I checked out, I thought I'd drop around to Monica's bungalow and make my resignation official, even though I expected Johnny had already given her a heads-up on my disrespectful and ungrateful attitude.

Naturally, I was worried about the implications of Paragraph Nineteen Sub Two, but they mostly had to do with depriving me of future income that I had no right to expect anyway. Taking a laser blast between the eyes (or, worse, in the shorts) was a sobering prospect, but now that I'd whacked a few balls around with her, I suspected Monica wasn't such a fierce competitor. I recalled her running to the net, her eyes flaring in anticipation of putting it away, but signaling at the same time she'd be just as thrilled to get one rammed down her throat, for a change.

I wasn't about to try. In fact, it occurred to me that this was one time I was hastening to her bungalow and *not* anticipating or dreading the thought of servicing her. I'd ceased to think of her primarily as a sexual vortex, because, well, in a manner of speaking, she was my friend. We had looked out for one another — not because of any mutual affection but because we'd found a way, albeit bizarre, to uphold each other's interests. She'd gotten what she wanted — for a while, at least — and she'd tried in her way to make my dreams come true. It wasn't her fault I'd wished for the wrong things.

I wasn't aware at this point that the Honeypackers were working for Arlen, or that they'd succeeded in documenting some of Monica's trysts with Merle. I knew them only as the tourists I'd judged to be from Milwaukee, and my only dealings with them when I was a carhop involved occasionally suggesting the removal of their Winnebago from our lot, since Farnsworth understandably judged it a proletarian eyesore. However, they were smart enough to patronize our coffee shop now and then, so, as I told Hector, I wasn't about to harass paying customers. If Donald Trump pulled up in a blimp-sized land yacht, we'd accommodate him, wouldn't we?

Anyhow, fate would have it that on this occasion Lucille and Woody were asleep at the switch — chowing down at Wendy's, actually. But for whatever reason, their surveillance was not in place when Monica's visitor slipped in, and therefore you have only my testimony to what happened next.

The bungalow window was ajar again, and as I approached the unit I thought I heard voices inside. Considering the sensitivity of my mission, I judged I should gain as much information as I could before barging in, so I lingered on the pathway and listened.

"Surprise!" Merle yelled, much too loud to be discreet.

Monica didn't respond, but I assumed she'd uttered a sweet nothing in a low tone I couldn't hear.

"Okay, I had it coming," Merle said. "But you've got to understand. I have a job to do. People depend on me. They expect me to be there, just like they tune you in every day at ten."

Again, her answer was inaudible.

"Can't we go on?" Merle said, almost too softly for me to hear. "It's been pretty effing fantastic, just the way things are..."

A long pause. I imagined a prolonged kiss. Then, Merle's voice came again, filled with alarm, "Uh-oh. Oh *no!*"

It wasn't a cry of passion, more like a wail at being stabbed. So I stormed through the unlocked front door.

I found them in the bedroom. Monica was stretched out cold. Merle was bending over her, overcome with huge, gasping sobs, her face wet from a sudden gush of tears.

"Oh, Monica, sweetie," Merle bawled. "What have you *done?*"

She was holding an empty champagne bottle she'd found on the bed. She waved it at me and started to cry again, wagging her head morosely.

I went quickly to Monica's side and felt her jugular with my fingertip. If she had a pulse, I couldn't feel it.

"Is she...?" Merle asked.

"I think so," I said. And it wasn't until just then I realized Merle was dressed in a superhero costume — blue tights with a big, yellow lightning bolt cleaving her generous bosom.

I went for the phone, but she stopped me.

"You must be Rollo," she sneered.

"Nice outfit," I said. "That work for you?"

"I thought you were in Malibu," she said, as if it mattered.

"Well, I'm not," I said. "You gonna let me make the call?"

"It was suicide, you understand," she said. "The champagne."

"Whatever," I said. "We gotta call the cops. Right now."

"I can't let you do that," she said, grabbing her trench coat. "There's someplace I have to be. I was never here. You'll have to take care of it."

"What have you got to say about it?" I asked.

"Just get her out of here," she said, buttoning her coat over the electric symbol. "I can't be involved. Take her for one last ride. To Malibu. What difference does it make where it happened? I'll see you're taken care of."

"And if I won't?"

She repeated emphatically, "I'll see you're taken care of."

Handing me the empty bottle, she said, "And take this. Her

stomach must be full of the stuff. It'll make the coroner's job easier. And *wipe it down* — my prints are on it."

"How do I know you didn't — ?"

"She must have known what she was doing," she said resentfully, choking back a tear. "To drink the *whole bottle?*"

On her way out, Merle paused at the door and shot back, in case I'd misread her threat, "Cross me on this, and you're dead. And I don't mean like on TV."

I BORROWED a wheelchair from Nigel's supply closet. I wrapped her in the snowball fake fur, put on her trademark sunglasses, and did her hair up in a turban. I didn't think she'd mind looking like Gloria Swanson for her last trip down Sunset Boulevard.

I pulled the Porsche around to the service entrance, returned to the bungalow, wheeled her down, and lifted her into the convertible's passenger seat. Perhaps by now the two of us were old news, because if anyone saw us, I never heard about it. Imitating art we were, she as the old lush star with me as the gigolo boyfriend. She'd drunk herself blind after an argument, and I was driving her to Malibu to dry out.

We drove west on Sunset with the top down, made the right turn at Gladstone's, and headed North on PCH. Off to our left, the full Moon floated in a crystal sky and dropped its glistening jewels on the waves of the broad Pacific. It was a warm, glorious evening, and if Monica hadn't been a corpse, I'd have been thinking about bedding her for real the minute we got to the beach house. (Okay, I did think about it, but I knew it was creepy.)

Unbeknownst to me, we were being followed by an unmarked police car. Merle wasn't taking any chances and had tipped her cronies at the LAPD that her longtime friend and confidante Monica LaMonica hadn't shown up for cocktails, and Merle suspected foul play at the hands of a gold digger and ex-con who coincidentally fit my description.

Just south of the Charthouse the road rises up enough to create a scenic overlook, and, noticing a few stars were starting to wink through the haze, I pulled over to savor the moment. Yeah, okay, it wasn't the best of circumstances, but since I'd chucked it all, I knew I didn't have much longer to linger in the lap of luxury. Monica's death surely made Paragraph Nineteen Sub Two moot, but certainly her attorneys would know what to do — perhaps liquidating all her assets to fund the cure for Keppelhoffer's? In any event, I was fairly sure I wasn't in her will — at least, not in any way that might benefit me.

We sat and marveled at the delirious lunacy of the Moon, and it seemed fitting to remove her dark glasses.

Sadness overtook me, and I realized I needed closure.

I had grown used to confiding in her effigy, so what was so different now?

"I wanted to tell you how I was going to straighten things out," I said. "So much for my plan. I thought you had it made. I just needed to rework my own priorities. Who knew it would end this way?"

My message was missing the mark. She wasn't getting it any better than the P.M. did.

"I know it's weird my talking to you like this," I went on. "But, you see, in a way, I talked to you all the time. After Felicia and Hector bailed from my fan club, you were my best friend. Hell, you were my only friend."

I don't know what came over me. Or — yes, I do — I wanted to feel a connection with her, impossible as that was at this late date.

I took her by the shoulders, turning her limp body and pressing it to mine. Remarkably, she wasn't stiff yet, but I knew I was one sick puppy when I felt myself starting to get hard.

I didn't see or hear the police car as it rolled up silently behind us, its headlights off.

I embraced her tenderly. "Goodbye, Monica," I said, and kissed her long and hard.

The police car's searchlight came on, backlighting us in a cinematic, blinding aura.

A Hollywood closeup! Oh, the romance!

A voice on the car bullhorn yelled, "Police! Freeze!"

Detective Cheryl Ralston approached us cautiously, her hand on her holster. Her partner, Rod Hewitt, got out of the passenger side, stood behind the open door, and leveled his sidearm at my head.

"Her lips are *still warm!*" I yelled, embracing a whole new reality.

"You're a sick one, all right," Ralston said. "You had the doll. But she wasn't enough for you. You had to get off on the real thing."

She doesn't get it!

I pinched Monica's nose, pried her mouth open, pushed my mouth over hers, and gave her a big blast of air from my own lungs.

"Jeez," Ralston recoiled. "Stop that!"

"Her lips, they're *warm*," I panted. "C-P-R!"

As I gave Monica another gift of breath, the cop started to draw her weapon.

"Stop it," she ordered. "You're under arrest on suspicion of murder and who knows what other disgusting shit."

Before they could read me my rights, Monica's body convulsed as if she'd connected with Merle's lightning bolt.

She emitted a loud, croaking belch.

The detective was aghast.

"Ohhhhhhh," Monica groaned. "What a fucking headache I have!"

Dumbstruck, the officer asked her, "You okay? You want us to call the paramedics?"

"Absolutely not," Monica said, coming out of her fog.

"Miz *LaMonica*, right? You want to swear out a complaint?"

Monica took a deep, satisfied breath and just smiled at me. "What have I got to complain about?" she asked sweetly. "How'd I get here?"

"Your friend asked me to take you for one last ride," I said quietly.

"Why, that..." Monica growled. "It's called psychotropic catatonia," she sniffed. "I was depressed."

You could tell from her blank expression that the detective had no idea what we were talking about.

"I wanted to give my lover a scare," Monica explained to her matter-of-factly. "So I got drunk. Dead drunk, in a manner of speaking."

Moments later, I was helping Monica wrap herself in a blanket the cops had pulled from their trunk. They were back at their car, talking on the radio and making notes.

"She has to know I won't give up without a fight," Monica said confidentially to me. "She has a big fundraiser at the Biltmore tonight."

"Maybe there's a way we can all get what we want," I said, seeing another chance to devise, concoct, and otherwise manipulate events for the better.

"What about *them?*" I said, indicating the cops. "Merle is wired to the department."

"They'll do whatever I ask them to do," Monica said. "They have a higher loyalty — they're *fans.*"

THE COPS FOLLOWED us back to the Palms, where I parked the Porsche in the lot and I recovered the P.M. from Nigel, who I'd finally figured out was her dresser (and probably her pimp when it came to Farnsworth, but I wasn't in a position to ask questions or make demands). I just told him I had to borrow her for a quick cover job and slipped him a few bucks.

The three of us — Monica, Pseudo Monica, and I — climbed into the back of the police car, and Hewitt drove us downtown while Ralston peppered Monica with questions about the fate of various characters on future episodes.

I sat between the two of them, bookended by a twosome no one else could book.

"Can't you go any faster?" Monica complained to Hewitt.

As we merged onto the Santa Monica Freeway, he switched on the emergency lights and floored it.

Monica briefed me on what she expected was going on downtown, and I told her what I thought we could do about it. I concluded by asking, "If we go through with this, if you get what you want, will you tear up our contract?"

"You drive a hard bargain, Rock," she said with a grin, proud she'd mentored me into becoming a more formidable opponent.

AT THE BILTMORE, a $1,000-a-plate political dinner was in full swing, a stemwinder for Merle's campaign. The well-heeled patrons all wore black ties or designer frocks, and several location television crews were panning the linen-covered tables in the ballroom for recognizable faces.

Bulldozing our way through the lobby with the two detectives plowing ahead in front of us, our brave little band burst into the ballroom.

Twin banners hung from the balcony: "CANTWELL FOR MAYOR!" and "CLEAN UP WITH CANTWELL."

Despite our sensational entrance, no one took notice, because all eyes were on the stage, where an overstuffed dignitary droned, "And now, the next mayor of our fair city, the leader in the polls, the people's choice to bring integrity and honesty back to city government — and a mighty fine figure of a woman — Merle Cantwell!"

Enthusiastic but cultured applause broke out as Merle appeared on the dais along with hubby Dennis and the ever-reluctant son Marvin.

No sooner had Merle opened her mouth to speak than Monica bellowed like a cheerleader from our place in the back, "Hey, Merle!"

The TV news directors monitoring the camera feeds in their vans outside must have done a collective double-take as they spied Monica and her rubber double — and in a wink, all the floodlights and cameras were trained on us. My arms were getting tired from propping up the P.M., but I told myself I had a duty to carry her through to the end.

"Yeah, it's me!" Monica yelled. "You double-crossing two-timer!" Of course, it was her genuine emotion rather than any justification in fact that rang true in that moment, since she was the one who was abetting Merle's adultery, and, as for two-timing, there stood physical proof Monica was the champ in that category.

A hubbub bubbled through the crowd, with comments to the effect, "Isn't that *her* — you know — *her?*"

"That woman is deranged," Merle shouted through the P.A. from her position of power at the podium. "Remove her from the hall at once!"

But no one was about to prevent a genuine first-class Hollywood star from having her way, and Monica boldly led us up to join Merle on the stage. When some heavies moved to block our progress, Ralston and Hewitt flashed their badges, and we had no trouble.

"My friends," Merle was saying solemnly into the microphone, "my political enemies are not above manufacturing the most preposterous kind of slander —"

Monica grabbed the gooseneck mic from Merle, twisting it like a rattler that inspired in her not the slightest fear.

"This woman," she said, indicating Merle, "who was *almost* your mayor, is a liar and a cheat. She's guilty of, of, giving me up for dead! Not to mention her brazen infidelities."

"That's ridiculous!" Dennis said, his eyes bulging with a rage that didn't know where to focus.

"Oh, yeah?" Monica sneered directly in his face. "*She* left my bedroom less than an hour ago!"

The crowd reacted, not in a nice way.

"Lies!" Merle protested. "You see? They're trying to impugn my character!"

"We'll have you for libel," Dennis smoldered.

"No, you won't," Monica replied, turning from him to Merle. "Go ahead. Show them your superhero underwear."

Merle froze. Dennis glared at her, growing more suspicious with every passing second, baffled why she wouldn't just call the bluff and unbutton. Finally, exasperated that Merle seemed incapable of doing the right thing, he stepped over to her, undid the top button of her blouse, and peeked in. Merle tried to push him away, but not before the high voltage hit him. Reenergized with new anger, he grabbed her collar in his fist, and as she shoved him away, he pulled the blouse with him, popping her buttons from top to bottom — and exposing the incriminating blue undies and searing lighting bolt.

He saw it, the audience saw it, and not a few viewers at home saw it.

But Dennis's fury was not yet spent. He charged back at Merle, grabbed the waistband of her skirt in both hands, gave a mighty tug, and came away with the skirt, flapping like a matador's cape.

There stood Merle in nothing but her blue tights — literally, a comic hero.

Marvin's mouth hung open. If he ever harbored the slightest Oedipal urges, they surely evaporated in that moment.

In a fruitless grab to regain some dignity, Merle took the mic, pointed at me, and accused, "She was sleeping with *him!*"

It's my moment. It's my chance to make it all right.

Stepping proudly to the mic, I announced, "No way! I was with her," and pointed to the lifeless P.M., "*every* time!"

The audience — and, no doubt, the viewers at home — had no idea what to make of this, but it didn't help Merle's cause, because, they surely reasoned, whatever it was I was claiming to have done must be true.

No one in his right mind would demand credit publicly for something so twisted and sick.

CHAPTER 34
LOOSE ENDS

Monica felt she was justified in applying tough love to force Merle out of a loveless marriage and a humorless career. She'd planned to retire gracefully herself, but her public attack on Merle didn't sit well with the millions of fans who derived their sense of social justice from the moral values acted out on *The Edge of Endlessness*.

So the network canned the greatest living soap star, citing health reasons for the sake of all-too-transparent appearances, and she had nothing to do but sit with us on the beach.

She and I hadn't exactly finalized our business, and, anyway, I had nowhere else to go. I couldn't very well go back to Felicia when I hadn't actually been with her in the first place. Oh, I expected we'd end up together, but at present I was still dragging my past relationship around with me — I didn't have the will to return the P.M. to the hotel. In fact, the more I thought about it, the cloudier the issue became legally. In terms of personal property, the rubber doll belonged to Hector, whose generous outlay I had never reimbursed. Then again, she was an unmistakable rip-off of Monica's showbiz persona, itself tangible property under a law that protects stars' rights to exploit their faces like trademarks — even after they're dead (case in point, Elvis). One would think the star's claim would trump, but there was the little matter of the clay mask Felicia had made — with Monica's tacit permission — but which I stole, Hector borrowed, and for all I knew was still in the custody of the doll maker.

I might make a buck by selling her sculptured ass to Farnsworth — who could easily afford to keep her in the luxury to which she'd become accustomed — but I risked being charged with selling him stolen goods if Monica were to turn on me later and I couldn't show clear title.

And giving her away just didn't seem respectful.

As I said before, I didn't know what Pugsley had been up to, but I'd been feeling his dogged presence in my shadow, and I wasn't about to give him any evidence of further criminal activity on my part.

So, for the time being, the P.M. stayed with us. Now there were three lounge chairs on the deck in Malibu — one for Monica, one for me, and one for her artful rendition in rubber.

As we basked in the sun and caught the sea breeze one lazy afternoon, strewn about us were copies of the trades. Some headlines: "SCANDAL!" "MONICA GOES SPLAT" and "NO MO' MERLE."

Monica didn't seem the least bit upset, and of course the P.M. was even-tempered as ever.

"Smell that air!" Monica enthused, then added with a sigh, "You know, I thought revenge would feel better than this."

She looked over at me and the P.M. Fortunately for my sanity, we weren't all wearing matching outfits.

"If you want out of your contract," she said, "the Michelin Girl has got to go."

"I've been thinking about that," I said, "and I have an idea."

You'd think, based on past experience, Monica would have been less trusting, but she gave me my head.

Monica let me buy a laptop computer and a wireless link, and I broke my long digital fast by tapping in from the beach house, easily achieving the first phase of my plan.

I borrowed the identity of Louise Jones from a death notice in a backwoods Tennessee newspaper, and in little more than an afternoon of skillful hacking, I'd given her new life, a credit limit of $150,000, and caused her to make a down-payment on a triple-wide mobile home.

Not trusting the phones, I met covertly with Audrey at Starbucks. You'd think that she, too, would be doubly wary of my schemes, but she quickly saw the justice of my plan and also its potential for more spectacular grocery-shelf news, bylined exclusively by her.

Merle took some convincing, but what other options did she have? She truly loved Monica, after all, and she was grateful for the chance to redeem herself. Her connections with the coroner's office further enhanced the viability and credibility of phase two.

Our favorite tabloid hit the stands that weekend with a stunning headline: "LaMONICA DEAD IN FREAK ACCIDENT." Audrey's lead read: "Based on an exclusive tip to this reporter, *Loose Lips* has learned that Hollywood legend Monica LaMonica had a fatal allergic reaction to a glass of rare, vintage champagne yesterday at an undisclosed location."

News directors all over town were called on the carpet for letting that one get by!

HECTOR APPLIED his superlative skills as a hotelier to orchestrate an impeccably tasteful ceremony at Forest Lawn.

I knew Monica would have preferred a small, private ceremony, but now that the feeding frenzy in the media had grown ravenous, I saw no point in not flinging wide the doors of the chapel. After all, she could afford it — and her public image deserved it.

Of course, the members of the old gang were there to pay their respects. One by one they filed silently past the open casket — Hector, Laszlo, Gracie, Nigel, Johnny, Jimmy, Verna, Ernie, and, of course, Farnsworth.

It was a fitting curtain call to a vivacious, dramatic life.

Some people commented on Monica's waxy complexion, thinking it a shortcoming of the mortician's art.

As I confided to Felicia later that evening, some of us were glad she didn't look more rubbery.

CHAPTER 35
ARLEN WEIGHS IN

Pugsley, here.

I have only this embarrassingly opinionated journal to offer as evidence of any crimes committed by Hemphill. He was my charge, and I was sure he was up to something, and maybe he was. But he fulfilled his obligation and turned in his manuscript. I can't add much more.

Not long after the events described herein, he and Felicia Ferrulo were married and the couple relocated to Simi Valley, where he assumed the chairmanship of the LaMonica Memorial Foundation for Keppelhoffer's Syndrome. He's a helluva fundraiser, from all reports. She runs a small art gallery in a local shopping mall. They're expecting puppies.

Audrey Skolnick got her claws into Hector Gomez-Ibarra, but, to my knowledge, she hasn't induced him to break any laws. (Nigel and Gracie are also an item, I understand.)

You see Jimmy B's name on the sides of all the buses, and he hosts an annual celebrity event for Keppelhoffer's.

Johnny Halo was fired recently when Clear Channel bought the station.

Dennis Cantwell filed for divorce after his wife of thirty years left him nothing but a Post-It note stuck to an empty champagne bottle.

Me, I've enrolled in a course called "Fundamentals of Directing" at UCLA Extension. I'm really looking forward to it, and I'm thinking of quitting the Bureau if I can find a way to make a buck with a video camera.

Maybe surveillance?

Speaking of which, the Honeypackers handed the last of their tapes over to me, pulled up stakes, and drove their tin-shack-on-wheels off to someplace in rural Tennessee. They sent me a photo postcard by snail mail, showing Lucille holding up a small-mouth bass. The message says they're having great fun fishing with their new trailer-park friends, Thelma Jones and Louise Smith.

It doesn't take a professional to guess there's some fraudulent activity lurking beneath all this, but I'm at a loss to find a victim in the whole thing, and, frankly, it took me way too long to admit I got better things to do.

There's one old gentleman, however, whom I can't help but feel sorry for. His eyesight got so bad they pulled his driver's license, so one day when I was by the hotel, I agreed to drive him over to Forest Lawn.

He stood quietly over Monica's grave for the longest time.

Before he turned to leave, I swear I heard him say,

"*Hemphill. I'll get you for this.*"

NOW READ THE SEQUEL - RUBBER BABES

In the second novel of the Rollo Hemphill Misadventures series, Rollo learns that failing ever upward isn't as much fun as you'd expect. In this hilarious sequel to My Inflatable Friend, *clueless tyro Rollo Hemphill becomes the youngest-ever director of a multimillion-dollar charitable foundation. Far too late, he begins to suspect it's a money laundry for sinister players in the Secret Government who are setting him up to take the fall for an international fraud. But his paranoia becomes most acute when he becomes entangled with a succession of women he calls "rubber babes."*

Chapter 1 - In the Valley of the Happy People

The happily ever after lasted about three weeks. If we'd had a honeymoon — I mean, if we'd gone somewhere on a real vacation — perhaps we could have extended our bliss by a finite number of expensive but mindless days. Instead, we bought a house in Simi Valley and went right back to work, practical romantics so in love no thrill of travel to exotic locales could conceivably add to the joy of our everyday experience of each other.

We started down the slippery slope of mistrust and discord on a Tuesday morning. It must have been about 7 A.M. Our mistake? The topic of our breakfast-table discussion shifted. Prior to that portentous moment, the content of our exchanges had been almost entirely and intensely personal. She would express a reason for delight, I would affirm it aroused the same in me, warmth would flood our forebrains, and, more often than not, our more sensitive body parts would swell — any excuse to hump as if every day was Wednesday. Or, she would express a cause for discomfort, however mundane or minor, and I would scurry to alleviate it: Fetch the aspirin, scratch the itch, linger with the foreplay, order dessert with two forks. I could do no wrong!

But this fateful morning we departed from that regime.

We talked about the weather.

"Think it will rain today?" she asked, setting down her favorite teddy-bear mug, meticulously prepared by me with Mocha Java knowing her digestive tract would absorb the caffeine, increase her heart rate, stir her circulation, and bring a sexy pink flush to her extremities. (The edge of a rosy nipple peeked out from the terrycloth of her bathrobe, confirming the Java effect and making me want to take her back to bed, of course.)

"It never rains this time of year in Southern California. You know that." I thought my tone was manly, congenial, helpful.

"Yeah, I suppose you're right," she said dismissively, apparently deciding to ignore the counsel of the morning paper as she laid it aside. "I thought there was something just as the radio came on this morning. I was still in a sleepy fuzz, didn't catch it."

"No doubt another instance of the media manufacturing news to boost ratings," I surmised sagely. "Any amount of rain would be a big story in this drought."

The downpour started at 2 P.M. that afternoon. No innocent drizzle this, pleasant as a surprise shower in a leafy glade in New England. It was one of those continuous Raymond Chandler *Big Sleep* drooling rains, a Los-Angeles-class monsoon that soaks the thirsty desert for days at a time, washing countless thousands of Starbucks cups down the storm drains and out to sea, and reminding the residents they live in the city that invented Mickey Mouse and film noir in the same era with scarcely a clue as to the irony of their historic coincidence.

When she stumbled in the door that evening, she was drenched—about as attractive as your proverbial drowned rat and with the disposition of a rabid rodent to match.

"You're so fucking sure of everything!" she spat out, as she shucked off her wet clothes in the laundry room.

"What did I do?" I asked dumbly, my shields down, not realizing a call to battle stations would have been the wiser posture.

"You said it wouldn't rain" was her truthful statement of the obvious.

"Obviously, I was wrong," I admitted generously, naively assuming that pleading *nolo* would get me off without a trial.

"You were so sure of yourself" was apparently the nature of my crime.

"Okay, I was wrong. Do you have to do everything I say?"

"Not after this, you can bet," she vowed, now provocatively naked as she peeled off her damp undies, a gesture that did nothing to help me maintain the attention span I needed to stay on message.

"I'm sorry it rained. I'm sorry you got soaked. But it wasn't my fault."

"You know, just once, if you know there's a chance you're wrong, why don't you say something like, 'You know, I'm not sure, but there's a remote possibility it might rain. Maybe you should take an umbrella. I worry you'll get wet.'"

"Anyone will tell you, if you want to be a leader, you should always make all your points in a firm —"

Land mine!

"You're *not* my leader!"

A long, icy silence ensued as she donned her luxurious, fabric-softened robe for the second time that day, tugging it closed at the neck to snuggle in its warmth or perhaps to make damned sure no part of her luscious flesh could protrude to inspire my lust.

Was I looking for disappointment? Sure. More precisely, I'd been on the lookout for it since that day we took the vows. Nothing in my life had ever gone according to plan or worked out as advertised or exceeded my wildest expectations. So, not so long ago (as loveless mortals reckon time) when Felicia had smiled sweetly and finally accepted my second modest proposal of marriage, part of me was suspicious right away. Yes, this was something I'd planned (indeed, plotted for, as you might well know). And wasn't it the juiciest end to be desired — didn't all the glossy magazines advertise it to be the thrill of a lifetime? Certainly, if that promise had proved even partly true, our marriage would have far exceeded my wildest expectations.

In short, when we wed, my head was spinning with the thought I'd be slipping it to this delicious creature every chance we got, my righteous ardor inducing only squeals of joy. But deep down, where fear alone could penetrate, I was sure I'd be the one to get the shaft in the end.

Satan is an old bugger, they say. But no educated person, least of all Rollo Hemphill, gives the beast any credit these days. Evil, we postmoderns suspect, is simply the absence of God, who like a kindly but demented parent goes missing often enough but can't be blamed for creating the toxins that ooze into the abandoned void. But the way things play out, the way events on this human plane unfold and entangle, you gotta believe either God has a fiendish sense of humor or, as Plato and a few other crustaceous dudes believed, He's got an adversary who is more than worthy, subject to certain POM-dependent variables. (Sorry for the jargon. Phase-of-the-Moon-dependent variables are factors we code cowboys invoke when we've run out of all rational causes for software failure.)

So I don't believe in Old Nick for a minute.

I just wish he'd leave me the hell alone.

Why, indeed, does strife exist in the world? If we know what happiness is, and certainly if we're lucky enough to find some of it, why can't we embrace it, hang out there, hit that note, and play a long, languorous *sostenuto* until the Big Coda?

Maybe it's just that God likes a good story. As my crusty English teacher used to grumble, "Drama is conflict, you knuckleheads! No one wants to read *The Village of the Happy People*."

So don't worry. That ain't what we got goin' here.

The third novel in the Rollo Hemphill Misadventures series is *Farnsworth's Revenge*.

BOYCHIK LIT

Here's my essay on the genre I call boychik lit - the male-centered comic fiction genre about young men with more chutzpah than brains.

boychik: boy, young man. (English *boy* + Yiddish diminutive suffix -*tshik*)
– wikipedia.org

Boychik lit is a genre based soundly on a less-than-serious worldview and a preoccupation with the exploits of young men on the make, who probably don't read much, but aimed as well at men of a certain age who want to remember what it was like to be young and on the make, and who have little else to do these days but buy books.

Women of any age apparently find boychiks entertaining in their sheer cluelessness.

In blog posts and book reviews, I've previously referred to boychik lit as kinder, hipper fratire. But fratire is a genre that many readers of both sexes find offensive, and it hasn't enlisted anything like the enduring and faithful following of chick lit. *Fratire* was coined by Warren St. John to mean *fraternity satire* when he was reviewing books for the *New York Times*. He needed to find an alternative label because apparently his editors refused to print the male-descriptive d-word that seems the most logical pairing with chick lit. Never mind that neither of the authors he was reviewing (Maddox and Tucker Max) was writing about fraternity life.

Curiously enough and yet hardly surprising, offensive material can be solidly commercial, especially in coming-of-age movies. How else do you explain the adolescent humor of *American Pie* or the hilarity of explosive diarrhea in *Bridesmaids?* I'm at a loss to explain the nuances that separate the only delightfully dirty from the truly disgusting, but apparently fratire got it wrong, picking up nasty and unfunny labels like sexist and misogynist.

I don't think boychik lit goes there. At least, I hope it doesn't. It's not about glorifying bad male behavior so much as puzzling over the consequences of bad choices. And chick lit seems to intend much the same thing.

I believe the first chick-lit book — if we're to talk of the marketing genre and not the literary tradition — was *Bridget Jones's Diary* (1996) by Helen Fielding. The tradition, of course, is a much longer thread. Fielding reportedly used Jane Austen's *Pride and Prejudice* as a model. Then and now, finding the right man was the paramount concern, even if today's independent woman may eventually decide it's the wrong question to be asking. The popularity of the genre broadened considerably with movie and TV adaptations of this and other similarly themed books, including *The Devil Wears Prada* and *Sex and the City*.

The term *lad lit* got attached to a male-oriented counterpart genre, mostly in the UK, although its defining work, Nick Hornsby's novel *High Fidelity*, had actually appeared in print a year earlier than Fielding's. Most of Hornsby's lad-lit books also had their film adaptations. A few years later, the HBO series *Entourage,* which had no obvious literary source, was hugely successful in depicting a cadre of young men on the make in Hollywood. The show seemed to be a kind of programming counterbalance to the demographics of that network's long-running *Sex and the City* series.

No matter what you call the male-oriented fare, chick lit has been by far the more marketable product. Mainstream publishers are fairly unanimous in their assessment that women buy books and men don't. A related assumption is that young men won't or can't read, presumably because they've been conquered, co-opted, or rendered brain-dead by the computer game industry or excessive self-abuse. I believe that one reason *Entourage* was so popular was because, besides a younger audience, it also pulled in mature viewers, the men fantasizing about what it used to be like to be young and on the make, and the women of any age delighting in the foolishness and arrogance of men.

But I fear that *boychik lit* won't gain much traction as a descriptive term outside literary circles. In this country's publishing industry, centered as it has always been in New York City, it's pretty much common knowledge what a boychik is. Editors and book reviewers get the joke, and they seem to understand how the teasing connotation of foolish striving motivates the stories.

In the wider world, readers might well think that a boychik is a cross-dresser or hermaphrodite. Sheesh. For such ignorance, there may be no cure.

But picking up on boychik's literal meaning, perhaps the prototypical work was Philip Roth's *Portnoy's Complaint* (1969), a confessional comic novel about a Jewish teenager with a now-classic set of neuroses.

In a sense, the male-centered novel has been a mainstay of fiction for a very long time. What is John Updike's Rabbit Angstrom but a boychik, a coming-of-age protagonist captured in various snapshots through the evolution of his manhood? And who is Dostoevsky's Raskolnikov but bad-boychik wrestling with his life choices and his conscience?

Perhaps the feminist revolution spawned chick lit as an alternative to male-focused fiction in general. But, high as the emotional stakes might be in chick-lit stories, I don't think of them as being particularly serious about relationships. The intent seems to be to satirize the dilemmas of sexual politics and, as in the male-centered stories, to ridicule foolish life choices.

The first Rollo Hemphill book, *My Inflatable Friend,* follows a formula that echoes the beats of the chick-lit plight. The male main character is looking for sex and is bewildered by emotional entanglements. He is a hacker and a slacker, clever and resourceful but chronically lazy. He's a dropout who can't hold a steady job. Far from being the hero with a single tragic flaw, the boychik is riddled with worrisome flaws, with one or two possibly redeeming qualities. The tone is observational and witty, often sarcastic. The boychik tells his story in a confessional, first-person narrative. And at the end of the novel, the hero has almost managed to undo the complicated mess he's made in the course of the story and thinks he has learned important lessons, which may or may not be valid.

Rollo's godfather was Peter De Vries, longtime *New Yorker* editor and the mostly unsung master of more than twenty male-centered comic novels. Never one to shy away from topics in questionable taste, De Vries wrote *Forever Panting* (1973) about a struggling actor who divorces his wife to marry his mother-in-law and *Slouching Towards Kalamazoo* (1983) about a confused young man who elopes with his teacher. You couldn't write that story today. Its topic is no longer funny, a premise that might have seemed outlandish at the time but is now just another creepy headline.

Another recurring comedic theme in De Vries draws on the hypocrisy and silliness he saw in fundamentalist Christianity, particularly in suburban church life. He grew up in a strict Dutch Reformed household, and his stories are full of references to the Bible stories of his childhood Sunday School lessons.

So, given the politics of religion in today's society, there's another topic of his no one will be tackling anytime soon.

The specific engine of comedy in a De Vries novel, I'd say, is the consequences of following lust. The enjoyment engenders the fun, the sin its painful and delicious complications and punishments.

If De Vries is godfather of the boychik, surely P. G. Wodehouse was its papa. *Right Ho, Jeeves* should be a mandatory course of remedial study for would-be authors of any male-centered comic fiction. Wodehouse offers what fratirists mostly lack and what boychik authors should emulate – namely, a hipper sensibility, class – what his protagonist Bertie Wooster would call "the real Tabasco."

Wooster is the aristocratic main character of the wacky Jeeves stories, and he neatly fits the role of heedless and misdirected tyro. Jeeves is his canny butler and sage advisor in all matters, from choices of appropriate evening dress to marriage-avoidance strategies.

As the social milieu of De Vries differed from our own, so did Wodehouse's, with corresponding effect on his plots and the engine of his comedy. In his post-World-War-I Europe, a large portion of the middle-aged male population had died in the conflict. As a result, older women controlled a disproportionately large share of Britain's estates and wealth. They ruled as matriarchs, at least in well-off families like the Woosters. Young men like Bertie were understandably not particularly anxious to grow up and assume responsibilities in an adult world that had obviously gone insane. Bertie's overarching objective, then, is to remain a boy as long as possible, avoiding both economic domination by his dowager aunts and marital entanglements with young women from suitable families.

In contrast to the boychik lit plot but running in parallel to it, the Wooster ethos can be summarized thusly: Avoid responsibility, romantic entanglements, and financial conundrums. Fear marriage and anyone in uniform. Pursue amusement, particularly if a practical joke will end in a "good wheeze." Fraternize with like-minded adult males who, despite their social standing, aspire to remain boys. Encourage food fights, but only with dinner rolls so as not to create a mess for which responsibility would have to be assumed. Coordinate rugby scrums in the clubroom, but only if fragile crockery has first been cleared. Solving real-world problems (such as romantic entanglements) by way of practical jokes and stratagems might not work, but it's always worth a good try.

Rounding out this thoughtful little piece, I'd like to make a few comments about literary style, which in flavor these days I judge to be too much vanilla, especially for my taste in comedy.

Every male writer with an ounce of testosterone owes a big debt to that other Papa, Ernest Hemingway. Without his example, how would James Jones, Norman Mailer, Hunter S. Thompson, or John Milius have known to pose for their publicity photos wearing safari jackets? Why, I bet they'd have showed up in some kind of wussy Tom Wolfe ice-cream suit! With a pocket handkerchief!

No question, the faithful adulation of Hemingway's literary style has done a lot for American letters. Before Hemingway bravely challenged every word's right to exist on his pristine-white page, popular fiction was mired in annoyingly baroque convolutions. Authors with too-precious styles such as Henry James and Edith Wharton spun sentences like brocade, twisting and turning them until their poor readers were so dizzy they'd be tempted to commit the unpardonable sin of putting the book down.

Speaking up for the plain man who wants not one word more than the plain truth, Hemingway argued for sparse, minimalist construction. Cut away, prune, snip, tailor — hack and butcher, if you must — until the reader's eye can traverse those sentences like a plow through righteously straight furrows. Write so the text whizzes by. Don't give them an excuse to pause, much less to think or reflect. They'll forgive you if they pee in their pants because they "couldn't put it down."

Better yet, remove all personal voice from your prose style. Adhere strictly to the same minimalist set of rules so that your prose reads no differently from the next author's. Spare the reader the tedium of having to get acquainted with your eccentricities. Give them what they came for — a good, forgettable story, speedily told.

Hemingway was, first and perhaps best of all, a newspaperman.

And it's in the field of journalism that his influence has been most beneficial. In news reporting, straight talk is just the thing, as it is in any type of expository writing, such as textbooks, tourist guidebooks, and divorce agreements.

But I appeal to all you English instructors who preach Strunk & White as though it were the new King James Version – let the young storytellers cultivate their unique styles and find their voices!

If you want examples, find some audio clips of sports commentator Frank Deford's radio broadcasts. His style was inspired by the likes of Heywood Hale Broun, Walter Winchell, Robert Benchley, and a host of other nut-jobs of yesteryear who probably got their knuckles rapped in school for not following instructions.

(Case in point, sentence fragment. No sin, my view.)

I can't know whether the notion of boychik lit will affect anyone else's writing. I do know that thinking about it has helped me shape the Rollo books. I've also used it as a critical perspective, and I hope you can see how a boychik's sensibility can be applied to the other stories I've included here. You can look at any story from the vantage point of a callow young man who is just beginning to take responsibility for the direction of his life, and as you observe other lives pass by and through your own, you can temper feelings of fondness and regret with an active sense of humor.

And, no matter what his age, sexual preferences, or social circumstances, how a man thinks about women may be the real measure of the man.

As to whether men read, I hope that continues to be a ridiculous question.

ABOUT THE AUTHOR

Gerald Everett Jones is a multiple-award-winning freelance writer who lives in Santa Monica, California. He is a member of the Dramatists Guild, Women's National Book Association, and Film Independent (FIND), as well as a board member of the Independent Writers of Southern California (IWOSC). He holds a Bachelor of Arts with Honors from the College of Letters, Wesleyan University, where he studied under novelists Peter Boynton *(Stone Island)*, F.D. Reeve *(The Red Machines)*, and Jerzy Kosinski *(The Painted Bird, Being There)*.

Find out more at geraldeverettjones.com.

facebook.com/geraldeverettjones
twitter.com/superscribbler1
instagram.com/geraldeverettjones
amazon.com/author/geraldeverettjones
goodreads.com/GeraldEverettJones

ALSO BY GERALD EVERETT JONES

Harry Harambee's Kenyan Sundowner: A Novel - *Multiple Awards*

The Misadventures of Rollo Hemphill (#1 - 3): *My Inflatable Friend, Rubber Babes, Farnsworth's Revenge*

Mr. Ballpoint

Christmas Karma

Choke Hold: An Eli Wolff Thriller

Bonfire of the Vanderbilts / *Bonfire of the Vanderbilts: Scholar's Edition*

Clifford's Spiral: A Novel - *2020 Independent Press Awards Distinguished Favorite in Literary Fiction*

Preacher Evan Wycliff Mysteries (#1 - 3) - Multiple Awards: *Preacher Finds a Corpse, Preacher Fakes a Miracle, Preacher Raises the Dead*

Stories and Essay

Boychik Lit

Nonfiction

How to Lie with Charts - *2020 Eric Hoffer Award Finalist in Business*

The Death of Hypatia and the End of Fate

The Light in His Soul: Lessons from My Brother's Schizophrenia (with Rebecca Schaper)

Searching for Jonah: Clues in Hebrew and Assyrian History by Don E. Jones (Afterword)

LaPuerta Books and Media

YOU MAY ALSO WANT TO READ...

Christmas Karma is an homage to Anne Tyler, whom the author regards as his literary mother. It's about the travails of a dysfunctional family around the holidays, narrated by an angel who has a wicked sense of humor. Main character Willa Nawicki is bewildered by a series of curious karmic events that literally ring her doorbell during the frantic season, awakening years-old resentments and stimulating ever-more-intense personal confrontations. These bizarre visitations include a grizzled old man claiming to be her father, who has been missing for some thirty years but now says the title to the family home is in his name — *and now he wants the place back.*

As the angel observes, "The surest way to invoke the laughter of the universe is to make plans, particularly devious ones."

This humorous novel is also a case study in entrepreneurship and the often zany world of consumer capitalism — inspired by a true story.

Mr. Ballpoint

Humorous Fiction (ages 14 and up)
Hardcover – Paperback – Kindle – EPUB – Audiobook

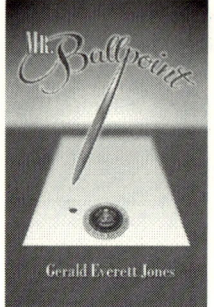

In 1945 Milton Reynolds introduced the ballpoint pen to the United States and triggered the biggest single-day shopping riot in history. Reynolds, an exuberant huckster who had already made and lost several fortunes, again became an overnight millionaire and then bragged that he "stole it fair and square."

Milton was a man ideally suited to his time— the post-war boom when the salesman was king and all of the rules had yet to be written. He was an old-fashioned, silver-tongued American peddler who would do almost anything—ethical or otherwise—to close a deal. His son Jim was a quiet honor student who couldn't tell a lie—even when he needed to.

Mr. Ballpoint is a father-son relationship story, told from Jim's point of view, about coping with Milton's outrageous schemes, then their sudden success. (It's a great Young Adult selection for book reports.)

"Forgotten history brought to life. If you ever wanted to know how to play the game of life and have a blast doing it, read *Mr. Ballpoint*. Perfect for our library and book clubs."

— **Deborah Vaden,** Manager of Libraries, City of Irving, Texas

"If only I had known about this marvelous invention before I started my writing career! No typewriter! No computer! The story calls to mind the old adage about pioneers and arrows. I salute Mr. Jones for his delightful and insightful tale."

— **Marvin J. Wolf,** author of *Rotten Apples: Tales of New York Crime and Mystery* and *For Whom The Shofar Blows*

Made in the USA
Middletown, DE
22 July 2022